LAURA

CLOVER SPRINGS MAIL ORDER BRIDES 5

RACHEL WESSON

LONDONGATE PUBLISHING

❀ Created with Vellum

CHAPTER 1

BOSTON 1885

It's more likely he'll be ugly, smell bad, and want a slave, not a wife.

The words she had said to Mary that night at the orphanage, when she first told her she'd decided to become a mail order bride, haunted Laura. They hadn't been true. Mary was happily married to an amazing, kind man. The last letter she'd had at the orphanage suggested Sorcha, too, was happy. Laura wondered if it would have worked out as well if Sorcha had not been a believer in happily ever after.

She chewed her knuckle, a habit the nuns had tried and failed to rid her of.

"Laura Murphy, land sakes, girl, will you stop lolly-gagging and put your back into it?" Wilma gave her a shove as her eyes sent Laura a warning.

Laura pushed the red curls out of her eyes, looking

frantically around the room for the reason for Wilma's warning. Then she saw him.

"There's my favorite girl. Ready for tonight?"

Laura kept the smile plastered to her face, her teeth clenched, willing her body not to shrink from his touch. He kissed her cheek, whistling as he looked around the room.

"Looks great, doesn't it? An improvement on the last place."

Laura nodded, knowing he wasn't asking her opinion. She studied him under her eyelashes as he walked around the new premises. He looked like a Greek god from one of her books. His charm and boyish good looks were what had attracted her to him in the first place. She'd been running errands for the cook when she'd bumped into him. Literally. He had helped her to her feet, apologizing profusely for knocking her over. She had fallen in love with him the moment he'd treated her like a real person.

She didn't like the look of the man with him. He looked at her as if he was a wild animal and she was his prey. Instinctively, she moved closer to Johnny, although he scared her, too. The devil you know and all that. She didn't look in Wilma's direction. Was this man the reason her friend seemed to be more nervous than usual?

"Aren't you going to introduce us, Johnny?" The

man's voice made her body tremble causing Johnny to glance at her. She smiled, hoping it would stop her husband from commenting on her terror. The man smiled back, but it only served to highlight the gruesome scar on the right side of his face. His skin was puckered around his eye, as if the blade had gotten stuck. She knew she shouldn't be staring, but her eyes wouldn't move away.

"This is Lee, my wife and secret weapon. With her on my side, I can't lose."

"I've heard of a rabbit's foot or a four leaf clover, but a woman?" The man closed the distance between them and took her hand. She itched to grab it back, but her sense of self-preservation kicked in. She held herself steady as he kissed her hand as if she was a lady in a Shakespearian drama.

"Good evening, Lee. I can see why Johnny's smitten by you. I am looking forward to seeing a lot more of you." He grinned at her as his eyes raked over her body. She took her hand and pulled her wrap closer, but it seemed only to heighten his amusement. She almost gagged as he moved, sending a wave of his musk cologne over her. "Johnny asked me to stay tonight to see how he runs things. We may be working closely together in the future. I shall see you soon. Very soon."

The man walked away, leaving Laura staring after

him. She tried to fight the terror engulfing her. There were people all around her, and yet she felt as if she was alone in the room with this stranger. Johnny hadn't even told her his name.

"Are you ready?" His question caught her attention. She smiled wider even though her cheeks hurt at the effort.

"Yes, Johnny. Wilma taught me the new game."

"Good." He moved closer to her again, putting his arm around her waist, closing the distance between them. She could smell cigars and whiskey. "You won't let me lose tonight, will you, darling?"

"No, Johnny." Her voice rose slightly as he pinched her waist. He was clever. He never marked her or any of the girls anywhere the customers would see. "Johnny, who was that man?"

"Why? Did you see something you liked?" His grip tightened and it took every ounce of restraint not to call out in pain.

"Of course not, Johnny." She simpered up to him, playing the part of adoring wife to perfection. She'd had plenty of practice pretending to be madly in love with him. She had thought she loved him once, but he had taken that love and stomped all over it. Not that she would admit it. She caressed his cheek. "I just wondered how he was going to be working with you."

"Coleman's got a couple of saloons and a few other

businesses. He's big, Lee, with plenty of contacts and deals to pass my way."

"He looks…dangerous." Laura couldn't help voicing her fear, although her comment caused Johnny to stiffen.

"Are you saying you think I can't handle him?"

"No, not at all. I know you are man enough for anyone. I just don't like the look of him. His scar frightened me." She fluttered her eyelashes. She didn't have to pretend to be scared.

"You'll get used to it. Now, forget about him. I got you a new dress. You'll like it. It's green, to match your eyes. I know you got talents, Lee, but it don't hurt to make the most of your other God-given assets." His leery gaze rested on her chest, causing her stomach to roil. Not again. Please. His eyes narrowed as they sought out her face. She'd forgotten to thank him.

Her mouth went dry as she scrambled to react as he expected. Otherwise, he would make her pay later. In all sorts of different ways. "Thank you, Johnny. You are so kind." She leaned in to kiss him on the cheek, but he turned, forcing her to meet his lips. She kissed him lightly before moving away. Not too quickly or he would get angry.

"Thank you, Johnny darling. If you don't mind, I'll go on up. I want to bathe and change for tonight." She forced herself to open the package he had given her.

As she suspected, it was beautiful. Green silk—he could afford the best. But she knew without looking that the neckline would be low cut and the sleeves almost non-existent. Johnny didn't fully believe in her gift. He believed in hedging his bets.

"I'd love to join you, but I have other business to attend to. See you later, witch." Her insides roiled as he called her that hated name, but she forced herself not to flinch from him. Any sign of weakness would excite him. The night ahead would be torture enough without inviting trouble.

Why didn't I take the job with Mr. Shepherd? She almost laughed at the thought that the old man was once the scariest thing she and Sorcha had to worry about. If only Sorcha could see her now. She always said her gift would be the making of her. Somehow, Laura didn't think she meant it like this.

Tears pricked her eyes as she made her way upstairs. The luxurious quarters only lasted as far as the customers went. Aside from the rooms used for entertaining private customers, most of the rooms above the salon were bare boards and plainly furnished. She was luckier than the other girls. She got a room to herself while they had to share with one or two others. Her room was nicely furnished with a big double bed in the center. The wallpapered walls and rugs on the floor gave the room a veneer of respectability.

This caused resentment and added to the reasons the other girls shunned her. Some were scared of her. She'd heard them muttering about witches. Others were jealous. She was Johnny's girl and they wanted him for themselves. If only they knew. If she never saw Johnny again, she would die happy.

Wilma came in to help her bathe and dress. "What's got into you today, Lee? You can't afford to make him angry. Not again."

"I don't know how much longer I can take this, Wilma. I hate seeing all those men lose so much money. Night after night."

"You don't make those men come into the saloon, darling. You're not responsible. It's their choice to drink and lose money at cards. That's between them and God. You have to look after yourself. You of all people know what the master is capable of."

"Why do you call him the master?"

Wilma stayed silent for a few minutes as she dressed Laura's hair. "You know the answer. It's the same reason I call you Lee. It's easier to call him that all the time than to forget it once. I don't want him hitting me ever again."

Compassion overwhelmed Laura. Compared to

Wilma, she was lucky. The other woman had lived her whole life as a servant to men just like Johnny. If rumors were true, she had worked as a saloon girl herself back in her early years. She could be harsh and strict and the majority of the working girls hated her. She insisted they bathe regularly and get checked over by the doctor. She wouldn't let them drink to excess, either. Laura had been wary of her when they'd first met, but over time she had seen the reasons for Wilma's behavior. Everything she did was for the protection of the girls.

Not that she was beyond giving a girl a slap, but it was usually for good reason. She didn't stand for thieving, drinking or bullying. She had been protective of Laura from the start. It was Wilma who had held her after every beating. She had massaged her battered body, rubbing a special salve into the bruises, to help them heal faster. Laura knew she'd have lost her sanity if it were not for this woman.

Johnny didn't know of their friendship. Nobody did; it was too dangerous. Johnny trusted Wilma with most, if not all, of his secrets. To keep that trust, Wilma was often cruel and harsh with Laura in the presence of the other girls. It was only in the privacy of Laura's bedroom where she revealed her true character.

"Wilma, what do you know about Coleman?"

Wilma stilled but didn't turn her face toward Laura.

"I take it you know him. Is he as dangerous as he looks?"

Wilma took Laura's arm.

"Lee, listen to me. You got to do your best tonight. Johnny's taken a string of losses and he is itching to make someone pay. Coleman's not his business partner. He's one of the men Johnny owes money to. The master knows he's in deep this time and that makes him angrier than ever. He's looking for a scapegoat. You can't let that be you. Your body has only just healed from the last time."

Wilma hugged Laura close. Laura let herself sink into the woman's embrace, although she was careful not to mess up her hair. She didn't want Johnny taking his temper out on her friend.

"I don't know how much longer I can live like this, Wilma. I'm not strong like you."

"You are; you just don't believe it, darling. Listen to me, Laura."

Laura's surprise at being called by her real name must have shown because Wilma laughed, her white teeth shining.

"It's a much prettier name than Lee." Wilma looked at her seriously now. "Johnny has gotten involved with some unsavory characters before, but Coleman and his friends make the last lot look like choir boys. He's nervous and scared. That makes him more dangerous than usual. So be careful."

"You, too, Wilma. If I ever get out of here, I am taking you with me."

Wilma looked at her sadly. "I ain't never going to be able to leave this life, Laura, and we both know it." Wilma pulled Laura to her feet. She walked around her, fixing her dress and hair just so. She opened the door to the bedroom, saying in a loud voice, "I don't know why the master wastes his money on you, girl. That dress must have cost a lot of dollars and you can't even smile. Have I not taught you anything, Lee?"

Laura caught the wink Wilma gave her before she pushed her out the door. Taking a deep breath, she walked slowly down the stairs, ignoring the daggered looks the other girls gave her. She guessed they were jealous of the dress, whereas she felt naked walking into the packed saloon. Seeing Johnny looking up at her from the bar, she quickly plastered a smile on her face. Like Wilma, she had a role to play in the nightmare she was immersed in. Unlike her friend, she was going to get out of here one day, no matter the cost.

CHAPTER 2

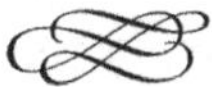

CLOVER SPRINGS

Paul Kelley paced back and forth outside the clinic. He moved his hat from one hand to the other, taking quick breaths as he moved toward the door and then away again.

The door opened as Emer pushed her head out.

"Have you made up your mind yet?"

"Sorry, Mrs. Shipley. I have business to see to." Paul turned to leave but stopped as she laughed.

"Paul Kelley, stop dithering and come inside. Doc can see you if you're too embarrassed to be seen by a nurse."

Paul flushed. "No, it's not anything like that. I just —well, I wanted… Oh, heck, this is hard."

"Come in and have some coffee. My sister dropped off some cookies on her way to the store."

Paul kept his hat in his hands as he made his way

into the clinic. He wiped his head with his forearm but it didn't help much. It seemed way too hot in the room.

"Paul, will you sit down? I don't bite." Emer poured some tea, placing the cup in front of him and the cookies on a plate in the center of the table.

"No, you don't. You're a wonderful woman, Mrs. Shipley." Paul's head jerked up as he realized what he had just said. He stood up so quickly the table rattled and some of the coffee flew out of the cups. He was a clumsy fool. He had to get out of here now before he made a total idiot of himself.

"Paul, please sit down. Whatever is wrong, Doc will be able to help you. I have seen a lot, so there is very little that would offend or shock me."

Paul reddened again, although he didn't think his cheeks could be so hot. "Mrs. Shipley, I need your help. I was wondering if you could help me write a letter. I want to find myself a bride. I'm not too good with writing."

Emer coughed as she tried to hold back a laugh. Of all the things she had imagined, this wasn't one of them. She immediately felt guilty. She had assumed from the man's nervousness he was suffering from a more intimate complaint.

"Paul, you know I would do anything to help anyone, but I don't know much about finding a bride.

My sister and her friends were the mail order brides in Clover Springs."

"Yeah, I know, Mrs. Shipley. But, well, I never spoke to them like I've spoken to you. You're real easy to speak to. You don't seem like one of them ladies."

Emer burst out laughing as Paul realized what he'd said.

"Oh, heck, Mrs. Shipley, I'm sorry."

"Don't worry about it, Paul. You're right. I am not like any lady. So could you please stop calling me Mrs. Shipley? I keep expecting Lawrence's mother to appear, and believe me, that's a lady you never want to meet." Emer smiled, trying to make him relax. "Call me Emer or Miss Emer, if you prefer."

Paul sat down again and seemed to relax a little.

"Why don't you tell me why you want a wife?" Emer kicked herself as he went red again. "I mean, what qualities are you looking for in the woman you want to marry?"

"Qualities?" Paul asked, his confused expression making him look even younger. If she hadn't treated him herself, she would never believe that the man in front of her had volunteered to go up against the Bainstreet gang. For all his youth, he was a brave man. *Apart from when it comes to talking to a real lady.*

"I guess I haven't really thought about it much. I mean, I've thought about getting a wife. I'd like her to be pretty, like you and your sister. My ma had blonde hair when she was younger. She's a good woman. Went to church every week until she got ill and had to take to her bed. She reads the Bible every night. You'd like her."

Emer wasn't sure she would. She'd heard a little about Mrs. Kelley and it hadn't been favorable. In her view, a Christian woman wasn't someone who just read the Bible and attended church. But she wasn't about to start talking religion with Paul, much less go against his beloved mother. Instead, she drank her tea and ate a cookie.

"You need to be a bit more specific, I guess. You can't put an ad in the paper asking for a girl with blonde hair." She smiled to take the sting out of her words. "What other traits would you like your new wife to have?"

"Well, I'd like her to have a kind heart like yours, Mrs.—sorry, Miss Emer. I wouldn't want her working in town, though. Ma and I have a nice little place. It needs a woman's touch. Been nobody to see to things since Ma took to the bed a couple of years back. She tries, but she gets tired real easy. I am not much good with housework. Maybe that's why she wants me to marry Ida Hawthorn." His lips curled with distaste.

Emer did her best to keep a serious expression on

her face. "I take it you do not see Miss Hawthorn as the woman for you?"

Paul blushed again, his hat going from one hand to the other so quickly Emer was tempted to take it from him. "No, Mrs.—Miss Emer, I don't. I usually do what my ma says, but I can't marry Miss Hawthorn. I won't."

"What will your ma say when you tell her you found someone else to marry?"

"She won't be happy."

"Is there anything else you would like to put in your letter?"

"I'd like children. A boy to take after me."

Emer smiled to herself as the man in front of her found an interesting spot on the floor. Despite her being a married, pregnant woman and a nurse, he couldn't look at her while talking about children. It would need a special type of woman to bring out this shy, sensitive man.

"Paul, why don't I write for you? I'll talk to my sister, and between us, we will come up with a letter for you. All you have to do is sign your name."

Paul jumped from his chair, reminding Emer of an overeager dog. "That would be just fine, Miss Emer. Thank you kindly. Will I call back tomorrow?" His brown eyes widened with hope.

"Give me a couple of days. These things take time.

It's a big decision to marry someone you don't know. Wise to give it some thought."

"Miss Emer, you won't go telling anyone about this, will you?" Paul looked down at the hat in his hands. "I don't want no one laughing at me. I would prefer Ma don't hear about it, neither. She has a way of knowing what goes on in Clover Springs."

Emer resisted the urge to touch his arm. She was a married woman now, and they didn't go around touching men. He wasn't a child who needed comforting. He was a grown man regardless of his youthful looks and big brown eyes.

"Paul, you don't need to worry about anything. I will have to tell my friends since they know more people in Boston. And Lawrence, but he won't say anything. Call back the next time you're in town."

"Thank you, Miss Emer. Your husband is a lucky man."

Emer's heart fluttered as Lawrence walked into the clinic. "I am a very lucky man."

Even after months of marriage, he had the ability to set her body on fire with a single look. She smiled at him lovingly as he closed the clinic door behind Paul.

Emer returned Lawrence's kiss before pulling away. "I just need to clear away these tea things. Then I'll get my bonnet and shawl and be right with you."

Lawrence took two cookies. "Mmm, your sister knows how to bake."

"How did you know they were Sorcha's?"

"Saw her coming in with a basket. My nose followed the scent of cookies."

Emer pretended to pout. "Here I was thinking I was the main attraction. All the time you were thinking with your stomach."

"It's not my stomach I think with when you are near, my darling little temptress."

"Lawrence. Someone might hear you."

Lawrence raised an eyebrow as he looked around the empty office.

"What did Kelley want? He seemed very happy when he was leaving here."

"Jealous?"

Emer gasped and giggled as Lawrence pulled her toward him.

"Not a bit. I know you are a one-man woman."

Emer kissed him on the cheek. "You say the nicest things. Paul Kelley wants to get married."

"Doesn't he know you are already taken?"

"Stop teasing, Lawrence. I'm serious. His ma threatened to marry him to some Miss Hawthorn. I don't think I ever met the lady." She glanced at her husband, who looked as if he was choking. His face changed from red to purple. "What? Lawrence, have some water. Was it the cookie? Are you all right?"

Lawrence burst out laughing, causing Emer to hit him. "Sorry, darling, but Miss Hawthorn? She has to be ten years older than Kelley. She looks it, too, with her beaky nose, scrawny neck and—"

"The poor woman. Don't talk about people like that. It makes you sound like your mother." Emer scolded him, but his comments explained Paul's desire to find a mail order bride. She wondered if Sorcha had any more friends in Boston. Paul deserved to find happiness. Emer looked at Lawrence, who still had a silly smirk on his face. She loved him so much she had to pinch herself sometimes. It was hard to believe this sort of happiness could last. Taking his arm, they walked out into the glorious sunshine. Emer locked the door behind her.

CHAPTER 3

BOSTON

The smoke and smell of unwashed bodies made Laura's eyes sting, but still she smiled. The room was almost full with paying customers. Johnny would be pleased, so hopefully he would be in a good mood later.

She moved from table to table, careful not to give any of the men individual attention. Johnny liked her to be visible, but he got jealous if she looked at another man. It was difficult not to do, given the place was swarming with men of all shapes and sizes. Even though all the working girls were downstairs, there simply weren't enough women to go around.

She smiled at a man who tried to put his arm around her, as her foot stomped on his. He howled as she apologized.

"Please forgive me. I didn't see your foot there," she

said, fluttering her eyelashes at the man as he hobbled off. She caught the warning glance from Wilma, but she didn't care. She was fed up with this life. Johnny had told her he would rather kill her than let her go, but even that threat had lost its power. She simply didn't care anymore. Life couldn't be worse than it was now.

Wilma's pinch didn't hurt, but it was enough to get her attention. "Johnny's called you twice. I warned you earlier not to annoy him. Not tonight," Wilma hissed through her smile.

Laura walked slowly over to Johnny.

"You took your time, darling." His eyes gleamed with anger, but as she got closer, she could see the lust, too. She did her best to hide the shiver of revulsion.

"It takes time to dress properly, Johnny. I didn't want to tear your beautiful gift."

He seemed slightly mollified at her answer before he took her arm and led her to one of the card tables. He sat while she rested her arm across his shoulders, the position arranged to display her cleavage to the best advantage. It worked, too, given the stares of the other cardholders. Shame engulfed her. She tried to adjust her dress, but a steely look from Johnny stopped her. His eyes held a promise that made her mouth run dry. Wilma was right; she'd have to be more careful than usual tonight.

Looking at the cards in his hand, she tapped the agreed code on his shoulder. She smiled at the other players, playing the part of the fancy girlfriend to the hilt. Only when he had played as she instructed did she allow her gaze to wander over the room. It still amazed her after all these months the number of men willing to bet their futures on the turn of a card. When would they learn the house always won?

As if to contradict her thoughts, a man sitting at a table on the other side of the room yelled his joy at winning his hand. *Walk away now while you still have the cash.* But she knew he wouldn't. She could see it from the way his gaze took in the amount of cash being played for at the next table.

At first, she hadn't seen the system Johnny used, but after all these months, it was so obvious. He let the new customers win small hands. Sometimes they won for two or three games in a row. Only once they were convinced they were on a winning streak did they throw caution to the wind and move to the tables where the prizes were higher. There, they might once again win the first or second hand.

Depending on the customers and Johnny's mood, they may even finish the night with more money than they started. But in the end, they always lost. Just as she had done. But they only lost money, not their dignity or their life.

"Lee, can you get me a drink?" Laura's heart almost burst out of her chest. She hadn't been paying attention, so she had no idea how to answer Johnny. Her eyes darted left and right, but the players were all looking at Johnny, waiting for his next move. He stared up at her, her clammy palms leaving a trace of damp on his shirt.

"Whiskey with water or on the rocks?" she asked, trying to keep her voice calm while her insides rocked. He looked puzzled. Little wonder as she wasn't using the code they had agreed on. Panicking, she played for time. Could she bluff? She decided to risk it.

"Sorry, sweetheart, I forgot, you never take it neat this early." Her voice shook as she spoke, her fingers seemingly massaging his shoulder in a loving embrace. She faltered over the code but got there in the end.

He sighed loudly, giving the impression to the other men he was sick of her forgetfulness, but his hard gaze told her she would pay later for her mistake. She prayed hard he would win, although she knew it was wrong to pray for a gambler. She was still sore from the last beating she'd received. She wasn't ready for another one. She watched, biting her lips as he played the cards. And won! She was nearly sick with relief. She'd had a lucky escape. This time.

"You cheated. I had the best hand at the table. You dirty—"

An ear-shattering noise rang out through the room, the gambling atmosphere pierced by the bullet headed straight for Johnny. The shot hit him first, the bullet passing through him before hitting Laura. She stumbled back as her body exploded in pain. Around her, panic reigned. More shots were fired before the darkness descended. She was going to hell. The nuns had been right; she was doomed from the start.

"Looks like she's coming around. Clear some space. Let her breathe." Laura opened her eyes to stare at the bearded face of a police officer. She struggled to move away but couldn't. "Lie still, miss. The doctor is coming. You've been shot. I'm afraid your friend is dead."

Why was the man being so kind? The police weren't usually nice to girls like her.

"Johnny," she croaked before she passed out once more.

* * *

SHE WOKE up some time later in a hospital ward. "Where am I?" Laura asked, struggling to sit up, her shoulder aching badly.

"Boston City Hospital. You were shot. You were lucky to survive. A number of people died. The police want to speak to you."

The nurse's gruff tone belied her kind eyes.

"Was Wilma hurt? Is she here?"

"I don't know the name of the girl who was killed. She had blonde hair. Was that your friend?"

Wilma was okay. Laura shrank lower in the bed. The police. What did they want with her? Who was the blonde girl? Marie or Maggie? Or it could be the new girl, Amy? She didn't know any of them well, but that didn't mean she would wish them dead.

What were the police going to do to her? Gambling wasn't a crime, was it? No, but fixing games was likely to be. They had no proof, and with Johnny dead, nobody else would give her up. Would they?

She lay shaking with fear, waiting for the police to come back. Johnny was dead. Did that mean she was free? To do what? She couldn't stay in Boston. She was a marked woman. Too many people knew she had worked in a saloon.

"Laura Murphy, I can't believe it. What are you doing in the hospital?"

Laura knew the voice. He'd said Mass every week and visited the orphanage. She wanted to pull the covers over her head. She couldn't meet his eyes. Her legs trembled so much she assumed he could see the bed shaking. She kept her eyes shut, hoping he'd think she was asleep or passed out or maybe even dead.

A nurse walked by and she heard the priest

speaking to her. Their whispers were too low for her to make out what they were saying. She didn't dare open her eyes to have a look. Maybe he would leave.

The seat creaking beside the bed told her he'd stayed.

"Laura, what happened to you? They said you'd been shot."

She ignored him.

"Laura, stop pretending you can't hear me. I won't leave until you talk to me. Didn't I tell you to come find me if you ever needed help?"

She opened her eyes. "Yes, Father."

"So why didn't you come?"

"I couldn't, Father. I am not the same girl who left the convent two years ago."

"What happened to you? Last time I heard, you'd gotten a job in a store."

"I met my husband in the store. Johnny Dawson. You heard of him?"

Father Molloy stared at her, the shock evident in his white face. "You married Johnny Dawson? He's a murderer, not to mention a—"

"He was. He's dead." Laura fought to gain control of her voice. "I didn't know, Father. He looked like a gentleman. We weren't married long before I found out who he was. He wasn't interested in a wife. I'm not even sure whether our marriage was real or not."

"Oh, you poor child." Father Molloy patted her hand, but Laura drew back from him.

"He wanted me because of my special talents."

"You are a beautiful young lady, Laura."

Laura laughed hysterically. "It wasn't my looks he was interested in. Well, not really. He believed I was a witch. Maybe I am. I wished him dead, and now he is."

Laura turned her head to let the tears soak into the pillow.

"Laura Murphy, you are no more a witch than I am. What nonsense."

"Mother Superior said I was evil. She used to tie my hand behind my back as I wrote with my left hand. She said the mark—" Laura bit her tongue. She'd said too much already. She looked around fearfully, but it didn't look like anyone had heard her.

"What mark?"

"I have the witch's mark on my body. I can't show you, Father. It wouldn't be proper."

Father Molloy didn't flinch. He stayed silent for a couple of minutes. Laura wondered what he was thinking. Was he going to turn her over to the authorities? They still tried people for being witches, didn't they? Johnny said they did. Of course, she knew about the Salem Witch Trials held nearly two hundred years ago, but she'd assumed they were history until he told her the last trial was in 1878. That was less than ten years ago. She could still hear his voice goading her. She had shared her story with him in the early days of their marriage after he'd seen the birthmark. She'd been so naive and trusting. She closed her eyes as his voice took over her mind. *You could have been descended from one of those witches. It would explain the foreign writing on the note, not to mention your coloring and the mark.*

"Laura, whatever happened to you, I am and will always be your friend. I will be back tomorrow. Try to get some rest." Father Molloy stood.

Laura kept her eyes screwed shut. She wanted to ask him to find Wilma and help her, but what if her friend had taken the chance to escape? If she told the priest about her, he may tell the police. She didn't want to get Wilma in trouble.

"I will pray for you, child."

He could pray all he liked, but it wouldn't do her any good. She was damned. She hadn't much of a future being a poor orphan in Boston, but now was worse. She was a trollop. A… She couldn't even bring herself to use that word. Tears fell from her closed eyes as she cried herself to sleep.

CHAPTER 4

BOSTON

True to his word, Father Molloy came back to see Laura every day. She was recovering well. There was no sign of infection now that the bullet had been removed. Her arm still hurt, but it was bearable.

"What's going to happen to me, Father? The nurse said the police want to speak to me."

"They want to ask you a few questions about Johnny. Who his friends were, that sort of thing. He had a large amount of gold in the saloon safe."

"I don't know anything about the gold, Father. Johnny didn't trust anyone with that. Not even Wilma."

"Wilma?"

"Wilma was the woman who ran the saloon and looked after the wh...girls. She's been with Johnny for years. Colored woman. He said she was a slave his pa rescued in the war." Johnny had said a lot of things. Almost all of them lies. The only time he told the truth was when he threatened to punish her for wrongdoings. Then he kept his word. Every time.

She stared at the priest, trying to work out if he had heard anything from Wilma. Her friend hadn't been to the hospital. Laura knew she would have come if she was able or thought it safe to do so. She prayed she was all right. *Coleman.* What was he going to do now that Johnny was dead? Would he leave her alone?

"Father, I'm tired. Thank you for coming over to see me. I wouldn't have blamed you for ignoring me."

"Ignore you? Laura Murphy Dawson, you listen and you listen properly. You are not alone. You never were. When you are well enough to leave the hospital, you are coming home with me. I am going to send you to Clover Springs."

Clover Springs. Where Sorcha and Mary were. Her friends. She let the hope live for a few seconds before it burned away. "No, Father, I am not going there. I am not the same girl I was when I knew Sorcha and Mary."

"So what are you going to do? Your husband, as you well know, was involved in wicked dealings. Do you think his friends are going to let you walk around Boston free as a bird? Regardless of what you think, they will believe Johnny gave you information. He may have just signed your death warrant."

"Good. I want to die. Goodbye, Father."

"How dare you? You do not decide when you die." She shrank further into the bed as the priest's face glowed with anger. He took a deep breath before speaking in a softer tone. "Laura, life hasn't been kind, but you have a chance to start over. Don't throw that away. Clover Springs has been good for Sorcha, Mary, Katie and the rest of the people who have moved there. It will be good for you, too."

He stood and patted the bed awkwardly. "Rest now and I will return tomorrow. I will accompany you to the police station, and then you will come home with me. I will send a telegram to Katie. The sooner we get you on a train to Colorado, the better."

CHAPTER 5

CLOVER SPRINGS

Emer pulled up outside of Mary's. She handed the reins to Ben, smiling at how healthy and happy Mary's adoptive son was looking.

Little Beaver held out his hand to help her out of the wagon.

"Thank you, Little Beaver. I am finding it harder to manage alone these days." Emer wondered how many hearts the young man standing in front of her would break.

"Mr. Lawrence shouldn't let you drive a wagon, Miss Emer."

Emer giggled at the Indian dictating what was proper to her. Her sister Sorcha had married a man with an Indian half-sister. The tribe had moved to the reservation but Nandita married Frank and decided to settle in Clover Springs. Frank had offered not only

Nandita's children but also her stepson, Little Beaver, a home. Emer was glad the boy had accepted.

Miss Freeman had told Sorcha he was bright and would be reading in no time. He just needed to apply himself to his schoolwork. It seemed the outdoor life held too much attraction for the boy. Little wonder, really. It wasn't that long ago this boy would have been counting coup as he became a warrior, married and raised a family of his own. That life had disappeared now. Thank goodness he didn't end up on a reservation. She hated to think of a free spirit like Little Beaver denied his freedom.

"If you keep frowning like that for too long, you will have wrinkles before you know it." Sorcha moved around to her side, watching Little Beaver as he moved the wagon. He would look after the horses.

"I was just thinking how different his life is going to be compared to his father or grandfather," Emer said with a last glance at Little Beaver. She turned to her sister to see her frowning, making Emer feel guilty for upsetting what promised to be a lovely afternoon.

"He's been so good for Ben. The youngster adores him," Emer said after greeting her sister with a kiss on the cheek.

"Meggie told me the other day she is going to marry Ben when she grows up."

Emer laughed at the little girl's antics. Meggie,

Sorcha's stepdaughter, might not be her real niece, but she loved her anyhow. She was part of the family she never thought she'd have. Not until she came to Clover Springs.

"Don't worry about Little Beaver, Emer. Frank is teaching him his trade. He's the one who insisted the boy go to school to get an education. He will have a better start than most. There aren't many boys who have both a trade and school learning."

"He'll need all the help he can get. There are some folk who will never see past the color of his skin."

Sorcha didn't get a chance to respond before they were interrupted.

"There you are. I thought I would have to send a search party to find you. This sewing isn't going to get done on its own, you know." Mary walked out, giving both of them a big hug.

Sorcha's sigh was so loud, everyone laughed. "Sorry, but you know sewing isn't my favorite occupation. I get blood on everything I touch."

"Why don't you read to us while we sew, then?" Mary suggested.

Sorcha looked like she was about to agree before Emer interrupted. "Actually, ladies, I need your help. I've been asked to write a letter requesting a new mail order bride. I told the gentleman in question I would write it and he could sign it."

"Who is it? Who's next to get married in Clover Springs?" Mary's eyes danced as she moved the infant she was holding to her other hip. "Don't tell me Doc has decided to get married after all these years?"

Emer burst out laughing at the thought of the single-minded doctor letting a woman near him.

"It's Paul Kelley. He says he's lonely and wants a wife. His ma has someone in mind for him, but he won't marry her."

"Good thing Ma Kelley is housebound and never gets to town. She'd have a hissy fit if she knew her precious son was writing for an orphan to marry." Mary snorted, overcome with laughter. She spoke again, mimicking the exact tones of Ma Kelley. "My son will marry the fairest in the land."

"Mary Sullivan, stop that at once. You don't mock the afflicted."

All the ladies looked guilty as Mrs. H, Mary's housekeeper, who was like one of the family, chided them.

"Sorry, Mrs. H," Mary mumbled.

Emer didn't look at Mary or the other girls for fear she would burst out laughing. Mary led the chastened group into the living room where the quilt was already spread out over the floor.

"It's beautiful, Mary. You have done plenty of work already."

"Mrs. H helped a lot, as did Martha. Elizabeth dropped over some pieces earlier with her apologies. Her kids are doing poorly and she didn't want to bring them in case it's something the baby could catch."

The ladies soon settled themselves. Mrs. H served tea and cookies but declined to join them. "I got stuff to do in the kitchen. I was thinking I might make Ma Kelley some of my special soup. That might help cure what ails her."

"What's wrong with Ma Kelley? I didn't want to ask Paul," Emer asked Mrs. H.

"A serious case of feeling sorry for herself," Mrs. H responded before leaving for the kitchen. The ladies erupted into giggles once more.

"I don't think I will be rushing out to call on Ma Kelley," Emer shuddered. "She sounds like she would be miserable company. Poor Paul. He's such a nice man."

"Davy remembers Paul's father. Said he was a nice man but timid. He let Ma Kelley order him around to the point he couldn't think for himself. They had a couple of boys. Not sure what happened to Paul's older brother. There was some talk he fell in love with a girl his mother didn't consider suitable. They eloped. Haven't been heard of since." Mary picked up her tea. "Who does Ma Kelley want Paul to marry?"

"Some girl called Ida Hawthorn."

Mary spurted her tea "Ida Hawthorn? Oh, the poor man. That woman has to be at least ten years older than Paul."

"Why would his mother want him to marry someone so old?" Emer asked.

"You wouldn't know, as you haven't been in Clover Springs long enough, but they are neighbors. Ida is an only child." Mary shrugged. "Maybe Ma Kelley thinks Pa Hawthorn will give his daughter his land when he dies. Oh, poor Paul. He deserves better than that."

"Are you still talking about Ma Kelley?" Mrs. H came into the living room carrying the unfinished quilt.

"I was just explaining to Emer why Ma Kelley would want Paul to marry Ida."

"There's nothing newsworthy about that. Ma Kelley has been planning it for years. Paul has tried to court other girls, but none of them lasted. Ma Kelley was a force to be reckoned with at one time. I could name grown men who wouldn't cross her."

"Mrs. H, you don't agree with Paul marrying Ida, do you? A spinster ten years older than him?"

"No, I don't, but it's not my place to be getting involved in other people's business. Not your place, either, if you ask me." Mrs. H walked back to the kitchen, leaving the women looking after her for a few seconds.

"Not sure what rattled her cage. She isn't always this moody." Mary looked to the kitchen.

"Maybe she wants you to marry her boys off. She might have a hankering for grandchildren," Sorcha said, eyeing the quilt dubiously.

"Well, I don't care what anyone else says. Paul asked me for help. I like him and don't want him saddled with a woman he doesn't love." Emer moved, trying to get her pregnant body more comfortable in the seat. "So do you ladies have any friends left in Boston who might like to come to Clover Springs?"

Before anyone could answer, they heard a wagon pull up outside. Emer looked out the window. "It's Katie. She looks upset."

Mary gave the baby to Emer. Picking up her skirts, she hurried outside to where Little Beaver and Ben were helping Katie.

"What's wrong? Did something happen?"

"Everyone's fine, but someone we know needs our help. Is Sorcha inside? She will want to hear this."

CHAPTER 6

CLOVER SPRINGS

Mary asked Ben to take Ella to play with the other children before she walked into the house, followed by Katie. The women inside looked up, their fear evident from their faces.

"Relax, everyone, there is nothing wrong in Clover Springs. I had a telegram from Father Molloy."

"A telegram? What's wrong with him?" Mary asked, her nerves making her voice shake.

"Nothing, but Laura is in trouble and needs our help."

"Laura?" Sorcha asked as Emer turned to her.

"Wasn't that the girl you were friendly with at the orphanage?"

"Yes, she shared a room with me and Mary. She said she would never become a mail order bride. We lost contact about six months after she left the orphanage. She wrote one time to say she had met a wonderful man and was getting married. She sounded happy." Sorcha looked at Katie, who shrugged.

"I don't know much. The telegram says she is arriving here by train. She needs to get married, and fast."

"Married? But she has a husband." Sorcha's confused expression mirrored that of her friends.

"Father Molloy wouldn't send her off to marry someone else if she did. Maybe she never married. I wonder what the hurry is, though." Katie glanced at Sorcha and Emer. "Oh my, you don't think it's because she has to?"

The women exchanged looks.

"This is Laura we are talking about. Not some, well, fallen woman." Sorcha blushed furiously. "The nuns broke her character years ago."

At Emer's quizzical look, Sorcha continued. "Laura wrote with her left hand. The nuns said it was the devil in her. They tied her hand behind her back, forcing her to write with her right one. She tried fighting back, but she never won. Eventually, she gave up."

"Yes, she had it tough. Tougher than most of us, because of the mark. And the note." Mary brushed a tear from her eye.

"What mark? What note? The more I learn about

that place, the more I am thankful I grew up with the Bainstreet Gang. At least nobody expected them to be kind."

"There were some kind nuns and staff at the orphanage. Cook was wonderful to us. She was especially kind to Laura." Mary took a deep breath before continuing. "She was there when the cleaning woman, Mrs. Murphy, brought her in. She was a babe in arms. The note on her blanket was written in another language. Some of the kids said it was because…well, never mind what they thought. It wasn't true."

"What did they think, Mary?" Emer couldn't hold back her curiosity.

"They thought she was a witch."

Emer burst out laughing but stopped at the silence in the room. The fear written on the other girls' faces frightened her. "Come on, ladies. This is 1885. Everyone knows witches aren't real."

"Not everyone, Emer. There was a trial in Boston in 1878; although that was some woman saying a man had bewitched her. It was thrown out, but it brought back all the stuff about Salem. Laura has a birthmark, just here." Mary pointed to her chest. "The nuns said it was the mark of the devil."

"And there was her gift, or her curse, as she called it," Sorcha added, her eyes full of concern.

"What was her gift? Could she talk to cats or cure

the sick?" Emer said jokingly, trying to lighten the mood. She hated seeing her sister and friends upset.

"It's no laughing matter," Mary said, her pretty face serious. "We don't believe Laura's a witch, but she can memorize a book just by looking at it. She only reads it once and she can tell you exactly what every page says."

"Oh."

"She's a real beauty, too. She has bright red hair. She looks more Irish than any of us," Katie said.

"Well, with a name like Murphy, the hair couldn't have been a surprise," Emer said.

"The cleaning woman's name was Laura Murphy," Mary explained. "She named the baby after herself. She died not long after Laura was found. She was killed in a freak accident."

"Don't tell me. That was Laura's fault too?" Emer's heart was breaking for the girl who needed a home. She didn't believe in witches, but she did believe in evil. She had lived it firsthand before she had the sense to run away. She was determined Laura would know only happiness from the moment she arrived in Clover Springs.

"We have a groom for her," Emer announced, feeling glad she had spoken to Paul.

"Emer, you can't be serious. Paul Kelley? He isn't the right man for Laura."

Mary shook her head, agreeing with Sorcha's statements.

"Why? He's kind, young, attractive and wants a wife. He's ideal."

"He's Paul Kelley," Sorcha said. "You didn't know his ma, but that woman would turn the rest of us into witches."

"He's not his ma. You of all people know that we don't become our parents when we grow up." Emer crossed her arms over her chest.

"Emer, calm down. Nobody is saying he's turned into his ma. Ma Kelley brought up her children in the same beliefs she shared. They had to read the Bible every night and attend church on Sunday."

"So what? Her elder son ran away to get married. She won't risk that happening again with Paul." Emer looked at the other women, but they didn't seem convinced. "I like Paul. He's brave and kind. It sounds like your friend Laura could do with a Christian friend."

"She could, but not one who will judge her and find her wanting. Laura isn't a church goer." Sorcha wrung her hands on her lap. "Well, she was while we were at the orphanage, but she told me she would never go once she turned eighteen."

Emer tapped her foot. She couldn't understand what the others were worried about. Paul Kelley was a grown man. His ma was an invalid. How much influence could she have? Her friends were wrong. Paul was the answer to Laura's dilemma. She knew it.

"She's not blonde, Emer. I thought that was the only request Paul had," Mary pointed out.

"He'll get over it." Emer stood, all thoughts of sewing forgotten. "Mary, I have to go. I want to tell Paul we found him a bride."

"Don't go just yet. We need to think about this. Wouldn't it be best for Laura to come to Clover Springs as a visitor?" Katie looked at each of the women in turn. "We don't have to tell anyone she needs to get married. Then we can introduce them and see what happens? If Paul isn't the right man, there are plenty of single men in Clover Springs."

"That's a good idea, Katie. She can come stay here. We have plenty of room. Davy won't mind."

Emer sat. It made sense to let Laura stay with Mary. She could get over whatever trouble she'd had in Boston.

"Let's make sure Paul is the first man to meet her, though. He's so shy; I don't fancy his chances if some of the other men find Laura attractive. There are so few eligible women in Clover Springs. Your friend could cause a stampede." Emer laughed and the others smiled at the thought.

"Now that we have agreed what to do about Laura,

can we please get some sewing done? Mrs. H is crotchety enough without me handing her back an unfinished quilt."

Everyone picked up a piece of sewing, even Sorcha.

"Has Ellen decided what she wants to do?"

Emer watched Katie closely to see her real reaction to Mary's question. Katie tried to smile, but she wasn't quick enough to hide the sadness in her eyes. "She is taking the stage to Boulder. She has a meeting arranged with a Miss Rippon. Miss Freeman was kind enough to write a letter of introduction."

"Ma will miss her and not just because she helps out at the boarding house. Ever since you both arrived in Clover Springs, Ellen has been like another daughter to her. I know how hard it is to lose your sister, Katie, but Ellen is very bright."

"Yes, Mary she is. Miss Rippon is one of her heroines. She is so excited. She can't believe she is going to meet a female university professor."

"So is she going to attend university?"

"Ellen doesn't know yet. It's very expensive and it also depends on what Miss Rippon has to say." Katie paused. "Daddy would be surprised to find out his little girl is going to a university."

Emer squeezed Katie's hand. She knew her friend was worried about Ellen traveling to Boulder alone, but she had to cut the apron strings. She hadn't been much older when she decided to leave Boston to marry a stranger.

The rest of the day passed pleasantly, and soon it was time for the ladies to go home. They left behind a finished quilt, much to Mary's delight.

CHAPTER 7

CLOVER SPRINGS

"Thank you, Mrs. H, for the lovely cookies and... What's wrong?"

Alarmed to find her housekeeper in tears, Mary dumped the cups on the table. She went over to the older woman and wrapped her arms around her.

"Please tell me what's wrong. Or should I get Davy?"

"It's nothing, Miss Mary. I'm just being a silly old woman."

"You are neither old nor silly. Let me make you a cup of tea. It's the Irish cure for everything."

Mary set the kettle to boil after checking the range was hot enough. She made herself take deep breaths, not wanting to admit how frightened she was at the sight of the formidable Mrs. H crying.

The kettle whistled and soon they were drinking tea. Mrs. H wiped a tear from her eye.

"Sorry, Miss Mary, for being cranky with you and the ladies."

"Don't worry about it. We didn't notice." At the look her words received, Mary smiled. "Well, only a little. We wondered what was wrong. You are normally so cheerful."

"I am just being silly. Martha Sullivan is a lucky woman. She has her children close by and now a gaggle of grandchildren, too."

"You'll be a granny one day, too. The boys will marry."

"Aaron and Samuel came to see me yesterday. They are planning on going to California. They want to have their own place rather than work for anyone. Don't get me wrong, they love Mr. Davy, but it's not the same as having your own place."

"Oh, Mrs. H. No wonder you're upset." Mary hugged the older woman, who had started crying again. "Are you going with them?"

"No, Miss Mary. I'm too old to go traipsing off into the sunset. I got my roots here. I just wish my boys felt like that, too." Mrs. H took a deep breath. "Look at me crying like a baby when there's work to be done. Don't mind me, Miss Mary. I got a family just like you said with you, Mr. Davy and little Cathy. I should be saying prayers of thanks."

Mary let Mrs. H get busy around the kitchen. Could there be a way to let the boys stay in Clover Springs? Wasn't there land available? Maybe the boys could put in a claim under the Homestead Act. Mary wasn't quite sure how that worked. Davy would know. Maybe Lawrence Shipley could help. She didn't say anything to Mrs. H. There was no point in getting her hopes up yet.

CHAPTER 8

BOSTON

The interview with the police took some time. Laura was glad Father Molloy had insisted on sitting with her. He had been so good to her, letting her stay with him and Mrs. Raines. His housekeeper had fussed over her as if she were a newborn babe.

Father Molloy hadn't let her out of his sight. *Maybe he's afraid I'll run off.* The police hadn't been happy when he said he was staying with her. He was only able to do so because the police chief was a member of his congregation. Over and over Laura protested her innocence. She insisted time and again her only role in the business was as Johnny's wife. She hadn't worked as a saloon girl. She did have an unusual gift and had used it to help Johnny win at cards. At first, the police had been skeptical, so she asked Father Molloy for a copy of his Bible and handed it to the police officer.

"Here, pick a reading."

"Any one?" The policeman exchanged a look with Father Molloy.

"Yes, any one."

He took his time choosing one and then handed the open page to Father Molloy.

"Laura, he's chosen John 14."

Laura closed her eyes. After a couple of seconds, she started reciting the exact verse the officer had picked. The two men stared at her. She kept going until Father Molloy told her to stop.

"You learnt the whole Bible by rote?" The policeman's tone was skeptical, but Laura was used to that reaction.

"No, I can do it with any book I've read. That's why Johnny married me. He knew I could memorize anything. It was helpful when he was playing cards."

"So you admit you used your…gift, I think you called it, to help him cheat."

Laura looked at her feet. "Yes, sir."

"Officer, that's enough. You and I both see how this situation happened. If Laura didn't help her husband, he would beat her senseless."

How did Father Molloy know that? She hadn't told him anything.

"You have your witnesses confirming what Laura said. We need to leave now. I have booked Miss Murphy on a train to Colorado. "

"We can't allow that, Father. We are investigating a murder. There is also the fact Peter Coleman is involved somehow. He's someone we want behind bars."

"This Mr. Coleman is the reason there are rumors her life could be in jeopardy should she remain in Boston. Frankly, this young lady has suffered enough."

"But Father—"

"Enough. We are leaving now." Father Molloy stood and, taking Laura's arm, half pulled, half helped her to her feet. "Come on, Laura, it's time to go. We will miss the train otherwise."

Laura followed Father Molloy silently, but her mind was working fast. Coleman was after her. Why? What could he want with her? *What Johnny wanted.* She came to a sudden stop. She couldn't go to Clover Springs, not if that man was following her.

Father Molloy handed her a small satchel. "Mrs. Raines, my housekeeper, packed some things for you. Your clothes weren't, ahem, suitable, so she picked up some other items. She also packed you some sandwiches, fruit and some water. There is a little cash in there, too, in case you need it.

Laura took the bag, tears pricking her eyes. She

rubbed them away, hating to show any sign of weakness.

"How did you know about Johnny, Father?"

"The doctors told me about the bruises and other injuries on your body. Wilma told me the rest."

Laura stopped walking. "You spoke to Wilma. Is she okay? Is she safe?"

Father Molloy's mouth turned down into a frown. "She is safe for now. She refused to let me help her. She said it was too dangerous. She told me to tell you she was free and would see you again someday." Father Molloy looked around them and then spoke again, but this time he whispered. "Wilma said Mr. Coleman has put up a reward for information about you. She said you have to get out of Boston as soon as possible. She doesn't trust anyone, does she?"

Laura shook her head, too miserable to speak. So it was true. She wasn't free. Johnny was dead but Coleman was waiting to enslave her in the same way.

"Wilma wouldn't see you because the police want to speak to her. I told her it would be best for her to give herself up, but she didn't think the police would believe she was not involved in Johnny's schemes. She did work for him and the other girls have spoken about her harsh treatment of them."

"She wasn't harsh. She protected me as much as she could. Yes, she shouted at the other girls, but only when they drank too much or wouldn't take a bath. She put herself between Johnny and those girls more often than I can count."

Father Molloy listened to Laura, but he didn't reply. He started walking once more. Laura had to walk fast to catch up with him.

"You don't think she was wrong to run, do you?"

"No, Laura. Her coloring alone makes her a target, never mind her occupation. I'm afraid not everyone remembers what they read in the Bible."

All too soon, they reached the station. Father Molloy saw her onto a car and waited for her to get settled in the seat.

"Tell the girls I will see them someday," he said, his voice slightly shaky.

"Father, I can't go to Clover Springs. What if that man follows me? I could bring danger to the girls."

Father Molloy looked grave. "I've thought about that, Laura, but I still believe you are safer there than anywhere else. The girls have good men who will all help protect you. Coleman will lose interest."

Laura wanted to believe him. She hoped he was right. There was something else she needed to know, too. It was now or never.

"Father, after seeing my gift, do you believe I am what they say?" Laura whispered after looking around her to make sure nobody could hear them.

"Laura, you have a gift. That is all. You are no more a witch than I am Satan. Put aside all of that nonsense and grab this second chance with both hands. You have a full and useful life ahead of you."

Laura couldn't speak; her throat was clogged with unshed tears. Without thinking, she stood up and threw her arms around the priest to hug him. He hugged her back quickly before coughing and moving away. He nodded to her as he left the car. His eyes were watery, and she could have sworn he was about to cry. She stood watching as he walked away down the platform until he disappeared from view. Only then did she take her seat. He was right. This was her fresh start. She sent up a quick prayer of thanks for Father Molloy and his housekeeper. Then she asked God to keep Wilma safe and look after her. Maybe someday they would meet again and she'd be able to repay her for everything she'd done. Finally, she prayed very hard nobody would follow her.

CHAPTER 9

CLOVER SPRINGS

"About time you came home. We've been waiting for ages. Ida cooked you a fine cake."

Paul groaned. He'd had a long day and wasn't in the mood for exchanging pleasantries with the Hawthorns.

"Sorry, Ma, it was busy out there today. Good evening, Miss Hawthorn." He looked around. "Did you come out here alone?"

Was she blushing?

"Miss Hawthorn's father dropped her over, but I said you would drive her home. It's about time you two spent some time together. After all, it's only a matter of time before an announcement is made."

"Ma." Paul had to stop himself from saying anything else. He didn't want to embarrass their guest but he had to take control of this situation now. "I'm afraid I will have to take you home now, Miss Hawthorn. I have business in town and it will be too late to drop you home after."

"Paul, you haven't eaten."

"I ate at the Sullivans. Now, are you ready, Miss Hawthorn?"

They drove in silence to the Hawthorn residence. Just as they pulled up outside, Paul cleared his throat. "Miss Hawthorn, I have something to say to you."

Her face flushed with what looked suspiciously like pleasure. His stomach dipped as he stammered. He hated to hurt anyone, but this had to be said.

"Miss Hawthorn, it may have come to your attention that my mother and your parents seem to think we are going to form a…partnership."

Her eyebrows rose, presumably at his use of the word partnership. He had to continue.

"I apologize, but I do not wish to enter into this… agreement. My heart lies elsewhere. I am sure a lovely woman like yourself has many suitors and will understand."

She just sat and gawped at him, not saying anything. The silence grew uncomfortable. "Miss Hawthorn, perhaps it would be best for you to go inside. Your father is waiting."

Still she sat. He was starting to wonder if he would

have to pull her off the wagon when the door to the house opened and Pa Hawthorn came out.

"That you, Ida?"

Miss Hawthorn didn't react to her father's question, leaving Paul to answer for both of them.

"Yes, Mr. Hawthorn. I brought Miss Hawthorn back from her visit with Ma."

"Want to come in for coffee, son?"

"No thank you, Mr. Hawthorn. I have some urgent business in town." Paul jumped down from the wagon and walked around to help Miss Hawthorn down. She still hadn't said anything. He tipped his hat at both of them and left, resisting the urge to push the horses into a fast trot.

I'm going to kill Ma.

He headed into town to cool off. If he went home now, he would have words with his mother. One thing his pa had told him was not to speak in anger. It had a way of coming back to bite you in the behind. He took his time trying to decide how best to handle his ma and her interference in his marriage plans. He pulled up outside the doctor's office just as Emer was leaving.

"Evening, Miss Emer, can I give you a ride home?"

"No thank you, Paul. I am going to the store. Walk with me?"

He nodded before climbing down and securing the horses.

"Do you have any news for me, Miss Emer? I don't mean to sound desperate, but I got to get married fast."

At Emer's look, he continued despite his embarrassment. "When I got home today, Ma had Miss Hawthorn waiting. With a cake."

"Do you not like cake?"

"I love cake. Oh, you're teasing me, aren't you?"

Emer laughed. "Sorry, Paul, I wasn't being mean. Sounds like your ma wants you to marry Miss Hawthorn and is doing everything in her power to make it happen."

"She is, and I don't know what else to do but bring home a bride. She won't take no for an answer. I think Miss Hawthorn shares her hopes." Paul turned his full gaze on Emer. "Can you do something to hurry up the whole process, Miss Emer?"

"I'm working on it, but these things take time. In the meantime, you have to set your mother straight. It won't be fair bringing a bride to your home if your mother is set against her from the start."

"Thank you, Miss Emer. You're right. I have to tackle Ma. Wish me luck."

CHAPTER 10

Laura huddled closer to the seat. All feeling below her waist had been lost long ago. Nobody ever said the car benches were so hard. She moved, trying to get more comfortable. Her shoulder ached, but in a way, the pain was comforting. She was free. From him. He'd never hurt her again.

Neither would any other men. She was done with love. Father Molloy told her she would have to marry again, if only for security. Colorado wasn't a state ready for a single woman, and there was a chance Coleman would come after her. They'd only met once, so the further she got from Boston the less of a threat she believed him to be.

She certainly wasn't going to get married because some stranger she had met once might chase after her. She'd never give another man control again. She wasn't going to fall in love again. *But then you won't have children.* She bit her lip.

Her eyes stayed on the ground, not wanting to get into a conversation with the other passengers. She could feel their eyes staring at her. Were they looking at her because she was a woman traveling alone or because they recognized her? *How could they recognize you? It's not like you are the only woman ever to have red hair. Stop being paranoid.*

The news articles had been a shock. Father Molloy had done his best to keep them from her, but she was bound to see them. She was glad Mrs. Raines had left the paper on the table.

Closing her eyes, she reviewed the article word for word. She was painted as a fallen woman. What had the reporter called her? The red haired Irish lonesome dove. She wasn't Irish. She wasn't what they called her either, not that anyone would care. Or believe her. Fact checking obviously wasn't high on the list of priorities at the paper. Recalling what she had read about Johnny's death in black and white print brought home the horror of that night. She shivered again.

"Are you all right Mrs.? Would you like some water?"

Laura opened her eyes to find an older woman staring, her eyes full of concern. She pulled her shawl closer around her shoulders, forgetting she was properly dressed in the suitable clothes picked out by Mrs. Raines. Her sore arm shrieked in protest. She sucked in her breath as the pain made her feel faint. She had to wait a few seconds to respond to the woman, which only served to make her more concerned.

"Mrs., are you sure you're okay?"

"I'm fine, thank you."

"Had a death in the family, have you? It's difficult now, dearie, but the pain will pass. I know; I've buried two husbands and four children. Babies they were. Not suited to coming out West, but try telling that to a man like George Ranshaw. He was my last husband. He thought he could find gold in the water. Silly old coot. Still, he was kind to me. Was yours?"

"Pardon?"

"The man you lost, was he kind to you?"

Laura almost vomited. How did this woman know about Johnny?

"Sorry, dearie, but with the ring and you wearing black, I assumed you were a widow just like myself." The woman pushed her hair out of her face, leaving a trail of cinders across it. Laura watched the black mark; it looked like the woman had whiskers.

"Oh dear, I've offended you. I jumped to assumptions. I'm so sorry. Judith, that's my daughter, she's always telling me to mind my own business. She says I talk too much. No idea why she'd think that."

Despite herself, Laura wanted to laugh at the confused expression on the lady's face. She didn't know anything and didn't mean any harm. It was a natural conclusion.

"He was killed. In an accident."

Laura glanced out the window, not wanting the woman to read the truth in her face. Being shot was an accident, wasn't it? Nobody plans to die like that, do they?

"Oh dearie. You poor thing. And so young, too."

Laura flinched as the woman took her hand. The sober expression on the other woman's face changed to one of understanding.

"Didn't treat you too well, did he?" The woman patted her hand. "You can see that by the way you flinched when I took your hand. May God forgive me, but maybe his death was a blessing. You are young and beautiful. There will be other men."

Laura jerked her hand back, tucking it into her lap. "No, there won't. I'll never marry again."

"You say that now, dearie, but just you wait. The right man is just around the next station. You mark my words. You were born to be happy."

That's how I know you're wrong. I wasn't supposed to be born at all. My mother didn't want me. She left me on a doorstep without even giving me a name.

Laura wished she could tell the old woman why she was wrong, but she didn't.

"I'm sorry, I'm very tired. I might take a nap."

"Yes, dearie, you look peaky. You mark my words, though. Life will look up for you. Yes, it will."

Laura closed her eyes and pretended to be asleep. She didn't open them when the other woman said goodbye as the train pulled into a station. It didn't do to let anyone get close. She hadn't trusted anyone, not fully. She was fond of Sorcha and Mary, but even with them, she had been withdrawn. Johnny was the first person she had trusted completely. She'd told him everything. Her fears, her hopes and her dreams. She cringed, remembering how he had laughed when she said she wanted a little boy and a girl.

A few hours later, she opened her eyes. She had drifted off and, for once, her nightmares hadn't been bad enough to wake her. She looked out the window. There wasn't much to see, only prairie. It was so different to Boston. She missed the smell of the sea. That was all she missed.

What was Clover Springs like? What would she do when she got there? Father Molloy had told her to stop fretting. The girls would look after her. But would they? Bit late to be thinking that way, wasn't it?

CHAPTER 11

CLOVER SPRINGS

"Paul, are you busy?"

"I just have to collect a few things before I set off for home. Do you need something, Mrs. Petersen?"

He watched as Sorcha bit her lip as if hesitating to ask him.

"Brian went out early to see to a sick horse and he's not back yet. My friend is coming to town and I was supposed to meet her at the station. Would you mind coming with me? Her bags will be heavy, and in my current state…"

Heat flooded Paul's cheeks as he realized what Sorcha meant. He looked around him, but there was nobody else about. "Of course, Mrs. Petersen. Is she staying here in town?"

"No, she's staying with Mary Sullivan, but I got my days mixed up. Mary thinks she is coming on Thursday. Do you mind driving us out to the ranch? I know it's a bit out of your way."

"Not at all, Mrs. Petersen. I travel by the Sullivan ranch on my way home anyway."

"You are so kind. Thank you."

Paul wished she would stop being so nice. He wasn't used to women smiling at him, especially pretty, married ladies. He looked at his feet once more. "I'll wait for you outside, Mrs. Petersen."

She looked very much like her sister. He hadn't seen Miss Emer since he'd told her about Miss Hawthorn's cake. He wondered if she had the letter finished yet. Mrs. Petersen would likely know, but he didn't want to ask. He took a rug out of the back of the wagon and folded it over on the seat. It would help to provide a cushion. The ground was rough and he didn't want Mrs. Petersen or her friend any more uncomfortable than they had to be.

Katie held her hand over her mouth until the door closed behind him. Then she burst out laughing. "Sorcha Petersen, you should have been on the stage. All those lies and you look like butter wouldn't melt in your mouth."

"I didn't lie."

At Katie's raised eyebrows, Sorcha smiled. "Well, maybe just a small one. Brian really has gone to see a sick horse."

"Yes, but Mary is chomping at the bit waiting for Laura to arrive. Today." Katie wiped a cloth over the gleaming counter. "I hope this idea of mine works."

"It will. It wouldn't be fair to push Laura into a marriage if none of us knows she wants it. Paul will be mesmerized by her beauty. You've never met her, have you?"

"I saw her a couple of times at Mass back in Boston. She's a bit hard to miss. She's stunning. I wish I had hair like hers. She didn't seem too friendly, though. I don't think I ever saw her smile."

"She was quiet. She didn't say much apart from telling me I was a dreamer. She told me that a lot. She got a very hard deal from a lot of the staff there." Sorcha looked at her hands before glancing back up at Katie. "We are never happy with what we have, are we? I would love dark hair like yours. Laura always hated her red hair."

"Wonder what sort of trouble she's been in? Guess we will find out soon enough. You better go or Paul will think you have been kidnapped."

"Oh my, I forgot about Paul. See you." Sorcha rushed out the door, leaving it open in her haste to leave. Katie walked over to the door, watching as Paul helped Sorcha into the wagon. Shutting the door gently behind her, she wondered again why Father Molloy had sent Laura to Clover Springs in such a hurry.

CHAPTER 12

"Is your friend staying long, Mrs. Petersen?"

"I'm not sure what her plans are, Paul. Guess we will soon find out."

They pulled into the station just as the train's whistle alerted its arrival. Car doors opened and the platform bustled with passengers coming and going. Sorcha saw Laura before she spotted them. It gave her a few minutes to hide her reaction. Her friend looked so different from the last time she had seen her at the orphanage. She was thinner for a start, and her eyes looked even bigger than usual, shadowed as they were with dark circles. It wasn't just her appearance, although the black clothes didn't help. Laura had never been full of the joy of life, but now there was such an air of sadness around her, Sorcha had to fight her instinct to gather her into a big hug. Laura didn't like physical expressions of affection, particularly in public places.

"I see her, Paul."

When Paul didn't respond, Sorcha looked at his face to find him staring at Laura as if transfixed. She hid a smile. This would be even easier than Katie had thought.

"Laura, I am so glad to see you. Come here." Sorcha put her arm around Laura's shoulders, but immediately drew back as her friend flinched. Pushing her gently back, she stared into her face. "What's wrong? Are you hurt?"

"It's nothing." Just at that moment, Laura's shawl fell down slightly, showing the bandaged arm.

Sorcha kicked herself hard. She must have hurt her friend, grabbing her into a hug like that. Now she wished they were alone so she could ask what had happened. Father Molloy had hinted at trouble. Sorcha couldn't shake the feeling it was worse than any of them feared. She heard a cough behind her.

"Oh, sorry. Where are my manners? Laura Murphy, please meet a friend of ours, Paul Kelley."

"Pleased to meet you, Miss Murphy." Paul's flushed cheeks and the slight quiver in his voice proved he was mesmerized by her friend.

Laura looked at him, but barely acknowledged his

welcome. Instead, she looked back down at the station floor. That was rude. Sorcha was about to apologize when Paul spoke again.

"Can I take your bags? The wagon is outside."

Without waiting for an answer, Paul took the satchel at Laura's feet. His hand reached for her other bag, but she held it closer. *She looks terrified.*

Paul sent a concerned look in Sorcha's direction before heading for the wagon. "I'll wait with the horses."

Sorcha said a quick prayer of thanks for Paul's thoughtfulness and a request for strength to help Laura get over whatever had happened. She wished Emer, Mary and Katie had come to the station, too. She had never known Laura to be like this. Usually there was a spark in her eye, particularly after a beating or other punishment for some infraction at the orphanage, but now those same green eyes were dead, void of expression. Sorcha was out of her depth and wished desperately the other girls were here to take over. *Pull yourself together. Your friend needs help.*

Seeing as the station platform was not the place to discuss secrets, she decided to be businesslike and unemotional.

"We best hurry. If I know Mary, she will have a path worn out waiting for us to turn up. Her housekeeper, Mrs. H, makes the best pies you've ever tasted. I don't know about you, but I'm starving."

"I need a bath and I am very tired. Do you think Mary would mind if I went straight to bed?"

Sorcha tried hard not to show her disappointment. "Of course not. We all remember the train journey from Boston to Clover Springs. A good soak and a rest in a real bed is just what the doctor ordered. Come on. Let's not keep Paul waiting."

They walked to the wagon in silence. Sorcha prayed Paul wouldn't start asking questions, but he stayed silent for most of the trip. Sorcha couldn't help thinking Laura's story was worse than anything any of them had imagined. It seemed to take forever for them to get to Mary's home.

CHAPTER 13

Laura perched on the wagon seat, swaying with the rolls as it moved across the prairie. After the crowded streets of Boston, she couldn't believe there wasn't a property in sight for miles. She concentrated on the scenery around her, not wanting her thoughts to drift to the man driving the wagon. Father Molloy had insisted she come to Clover Springs and get married. He hadn't specified to whom. He had probably left that to Mary and Sorcha to decide. Not that it mattered. She wasn't getting married to anyone.

Maybe that's why Mr. Kelley had collected her. Was he the groom they'd chosen? She edged away from him, though she couldn't move far for fear of falling off the wagon. The extra space should have made her feel better, but it didn't. She wasn't indifferent to this male stranger, which made her nervous. She should know better, given her history with men.

Mr. Kelley wasn't as handsome as Johnny, but he was quite attractive. She'd have to be a nun not to see that. She was tall and not used to looking up at the men she met, but she only came to his shoulders. Broad shoulders. He had to bend his head to talk to her, making her feel petite. He wasn't sporting the usual beard and whiskers but was clean-shaven, although a dark shadow hinted on his jaw.

It wasn't just his physical appearance that had her senses on high alert. She loved his voice. It was deep and velvety and somehow she got the feeling she could trust him. A man she'd only just met. She sat straighter. She'd trusted a man before and look at the mess that had left her in. Driven almost halfway across the country, away from the only life she had ever known.

Stop it, Laura. You are going to be with your friends. They won't let you starve.

She was glad Sorcha had given up trying to make conversation. She had seen the shock in her friend's eyes as they came face to face at the station. She knew Sorcha had questions. Mary would have them too. How much had Father Molloy told them? How she wished he had come with her. She almost laughed out loud. She, who had pretty much given up on God, was wishing a priest had travelled with her to Clover Springs. *For what? Protection?*

"THAT'S the Sullivan ranch up above, Miss Murphy. Fine big house. You will feel much better once Mrs. H starts looking after you. She is the best cook for miles around," Paul said softly. He couldn't explain his need to prove to this lady she would only find kindness at the Sullivan ranch. She reminded him of a puppy he'd once brought home. It was a skinny little thing, its bones sticking out through what was left of its fur. Someone had mistreated it badly, and as a result, it tried to bite anyone who came close. It had taken him days to get the animal to trust him. But eventually Spots, as he'd named him, had taken to following him everywhere.

He swallowed hard, remembering how his mother had found the dog and insisted he train it to help round up the cattle. He had argued, but to no avail. Spots had become his father's working dog. He was killed soon after when something spooked the cattle and he got trampled.

What are you doing comparing a beautiful woman to a dog? She was stunning to look at. He had never seen hair her color before, but it suited her. He had noted her pinching her lips before she saw them. He'd thought at first she found something distasteful in Clover Springs, but upon closer inspection, he had seen the fear in her eyes. He never would've guessed she was the woman Sorcha had been waiting for.

When he had heard her whimper as Sorcha hugged her, his insides had turned over. He wanted to trash whomever had hurt her. He wasn't a violent man. He had been shot riding with the posse, not because he believed in glory, but because Clover Springs was in trouble and needed protecting. It was his duty to ride out with the sheriff.

People had been surprised he volunteered for the posse. Having grown up in Clover Springs, he'd never shaken the reputation of being a coward. If he closed his eyes, he could hear the children calling him a mama's boy just because he walked away from a fight more often than not. He didn't care what people thought of him; there was nothing to gain by using your fists on another person. Yet if the man who had hurt this stranger stood in front of him, he would beat him until he couldn't stand.

Paul flexed his fists as he fought to control the anger consuming him. He wasn't used to feeling this way, but this woman attracted him more than just physically. He felt a pull toward her that he couldn't explain to himself, never mind anyone else. It was silly.

She wasn't alone. Mary Sullivan and Sorcha Petersen had been her friends for years. They would look after her. Yet he didn't want to leave her.

He pulled up slowly as the door opened and Mary came running out. Despite her advanced state of pregnancy, Sorcha almost jumped off the wagon in her haste to meet Mary. He guessed she wanted to warn the other woman not to hug Miss Murphy for fear of hurting her. Whatever her reason, Sorcha had left him alone with the red-haired woman for a minute. He seized his chance.

As he helped her down from the wagon, he whispered, "Miss Murphy, I don't know you, and I have no idea what you've been through, but Clover Springs and the people in it will heal your wounds if you let them. Let the past go. Trust your friends. We'll look after you."

He caught the surprise in her eyes before she drew the shutters back down. *We'll look after you.* He had put himself in there with her friends. She would think him a lunatic.

He stood watching her as she walked slowly over to where Mary and Sorcha stood, concern etched on their faces. Mary took a hold of her good arm and, together, the women walked into the house. Just before she reached the door, Laura glanced back at him. He smiled despite the fact she didn't.

He picked up her bags and walked up to the door as Mrs. H came out. "Mighty quiet reunion for girls who haven't seen each other in a couple of years, don't you think?"

"Yes, Ma'am. Where do you want these bags?"

"Could you carry them to her room for me, Paul? I have pie waiting for you in the kitchen."

"You don't need to pay me in pie, Mrs. H, although I would never say no to your cooking. You've got to be the best cook for miles around."

"You may not say much, Paul Kelley, but when you do open your mouth, it's always something nice." Mrs. H walked in front of him, leading the way to the bedroom. There was no sign of Miss Murphy. He guessed the ladies would have taken her into the sitting room. Walking into the bedroom, he spotted the tub, the steaming water looking so inviting. His mind wandered despite his best intentions. He almost dropped the cases in his haste to get out of the room before he embarrassed himself. It was bad enough he was thinking of Miss Murphy in the bath without letting Mrs. H know the direction his thoughts had taken.

CHAPTER 14

"Sit down, Laura. Make yourself at home. It's so good to see you." Mary tried to keep talking to dispel the awkward silence but, for once, she was lost for words. She couldn't get over the difference in Laura. It looked like the girl was trying to disappear inside her own skin.

"Thank you, Mary, you are very kind."

The dull, listless voice only heightened Mary's concern. She exchanged a look with Sorcha.

"Laura, Mrs. H has a hot bath waiting for you. I can remember how tired and grimy I was after that train journey. Would you like something to eat first?"

"No thank you, Mary."

She noticed Laura didn't even look around the room but just stood there. "Do you want any help?

You've hurt your arm. I can help you get undressed if you want."

"Thank you, Mary, but I can manage." Laura looked to the door. "Can you please show me to my room?"

"Laura, it's us. Me and Mary. We're your friends. Can't you tell us what happened? What we can do to make it better?" Sorcha's voice quivered with emotion.

"You can't help me. Nobody can. I tried telling Father Molloy, but he insisted I come here." Laura's flat voice made Mary want to cry.

"Come along, Miss Murphy. Your bath is getting cold. There's coffee and pie in the kitchen, Miss Mary. You and Miss Sorcha can see to yourselves. I'll help Miss Murphy."

Never was Mary so relieved to have Mrs. H around. The older woman would know what to do.

Mary and Sorcha waited as Laura followed Mrs. H out of the room, still clutching her bag in her hand.

"Oh, Sorcha, what happened to her? She looks so miserable."

"She's so thin and her arm is hurting her a lot. I saw her wincing when she thought nobody was looking. "

"I wanted to give her a big hug, but Laura was never into cuddles. I can't understand why she isn't talking, though. This is us. We know what the orphanage was like. We used to share everything."

"No, Mary, you and I shared everything. Laura was

always a bit of a loner. Do you remember what she said to you when you were leaving to marry Davy?"

Mary smiled at the memory. "She was so wrong, wasn't she? Davy couldn't be less like she thought my mail order husband would be. Did you see she has a ring on her finger? Looks like she got married. Maybe she's running away from her husband? Oh, Sorcha, she looks so fragile."

"Don't cry. Cathy will get upset."

"Cathy's only ten months old. All she cares about is getting fed and her bottom being dry."

"She gives the best cuddles, though. Come on. Let's go get some pie before Paul eats it all."

"Paul Kelley. How could I forget he was here? Katie's plan isn't going to work now. There's no way any man would look at Laura and see her as wife material. Not now."

"She couldn't be wife material anyway if she's married. I guess there is more to Laura's story, but we just have to be patient. She'll tell us in her own time."

Mary hoped Sorcha was right as she followed her into the kitchen.

CHAPTER 15

Laura followed the older woman as she led the way up the stairs to what she figured must be the guest bedroom. The house was lovely, bigger than she thought it would be. Mary looked happy, too. *Well, she did until she saw me.*

"Now, Miss Laura. You don't mind me calling you that do you? I call all Miss Mary's friends by their first name. Paul put your bag on the bed. Would you like me to unpack for you?"

Laura was about to say no, but the housekeeper had the bag open and was unpacking already. She watched her closely, looking for a reaction to the lack of clothing, but there wasn't any. She was glad Mrs. Raines hadn't packed any of the clothes Johnny had bought for her.

Laura let her shawl fall onto the bed. Her arm was

aching. The water looked great, but she wasn't sure she would be able to undo all her buttons.

"Don't stand there all day. The water will get cold. If you're shy, go behind the screen over there. I'll turn my back, but I can't leave you to it. There's no way you can wash your hair with your arm busted up like that."

"Could you help me with my buttons please?"

"Of course I can." Mrs. H started opening the top button.

Laura tried her best to hold still when the other woman touched her, but she couldn't help flinching.

"Nobody is going to hurt you anymore. You listen to me now. You are safe here, girl. No way is Miss Mary or Mr. Davy going to let anyone at you. Even if they did, and they won't, nobody is going to get past me."

Laura swallowed hard. She desperately wanted to believe the housekeeper, but she hadn't seen the mark yet. She also didn't know anything about her other than she was an orphan. An unwanted child. And adult.

"Miss Mary told me a little about what you went through at the orphanage. I never heard anything so stupid in my life. Your hair is beautiful. God made you the way you are. Nobody else had anything to do with it." Mrs. H undressed Laura as she spoke. She eased the bandage gently off her arm. "You best let Miss

Emer have a look at that wound. It looks clean enough, but I'm no doctor."

"You have a woman doctor?" Despite her vow of silence, Laura's curiosity won.

"No, girl, this is Colorado. We aren't that advanced. Not yet anyway. Miss Emer, she's a nurse. A mighty good one, too. She came to Clover Springs about eighteen months ago, looking for Miss Sorcha. They're sisters, but guess you knew that already."

"Sorcha found her sister? So she did exist. Mother Superior wasn't being nasty."

"From what I know of that woman, she is never anything but nasty. Yes, Miss Emer and Miss Sorcha found each other. They look alike, too, but guess you haven't met Miss Emer yet."

"Did Sorcha find her mother, too?"

"Yes, Miss Laura." Something in the housekeeper's tone made Laura look at her. She caught the look of distaste on the housekeeper's face. Was that because of Sorcha's mother or because she had just noticed the mark? Laura tried to cover her chest with her arm.

"Don't think you should be getting that arm wet, Miss Laura. Now let me wash your hair. You might want to wait for Miss Sorcha to tell you about her mother. It's not a nice story."

The distaste hadn't been aimed at her, but at the woman who had abandoned Sorcha. Laura hoped her friend hadn't been badly hurt meeting the woman after all those years.

"Miss Laura, your hair is the nicest color I ever saw."

Laura didn't believe her. She was just being nice. She got into the bath gingerly, the older woman helping her. It took a little while but, eventually, Laura relaxed. The combination of hot water and Mrs. H's soothing fingers as she massaged her hair was too good. She lay in the water with her eyes closed.

"Come on now, Miss Laura, you best get out before you catch a chill. I don't want Miss Mary to think I've mistreated you."

Mrs. H dried her off as if she was a baby. She didn't say anything, but Laura could feel her warmth and caring. It was a balm to her soul. She spent ages brushing out Laura's long hair before winding it up in a cloth.

"Now you will be able to rest without worrying about your wet hair." Mrs. H moved about the room, picking up the dirty clothes. "I bet you feel a lot better now. Would you like something to eat or do you want to have a rest first?"

"I'm very tired. Would it be okay if I lay down for a while?"

"You do whatever you want, Miss Laura. Nobody here is going to tell you what to do," Mrs. H said gently, her eyes full of concern. Laura didn't see any sign of condemnation. It surprised her, given the woman must have seen the mark.

"What about the bath?"

"Leave that be. Later, Aaron or Samuel will help me empty it. They are my boys." Mrs. H moved nearer the bed to help Laura pull the quilt back. "You close your eyes and rest. You look like you haven't had a good night's sleep in a long time."

"Not since I met Johnny." Laura clamped her hand over her mouth. Why had she mentioned his name?

"You shut your eyes and rest now. Don't worry about Johnny or anyone else." Mrs. H plumped up the pillows as Laura got into bed. She lay back. The housekeeper pushed some stray hair out of her eyes before placing a gentle kiss on her forehead. "Rest easy, child. You are safe here."

The door to the room closed behind the housekeeper, leaving Laura lying in the bed, her fingers touching the spot where Mrs. H had kissed her. She couldn't ever remember anyone being so kind or tender with her. Closing her eyes, she sank into a dreamless sleep.

CHAPTER 16

"Where's Laura, Mrs. H?"

Mrs. Higgins closed the kitchen door behind her. "She's sleeping, Miss Mary. You leave her be now. That child's been through the wars."

"Child? She's almost the same age as me, Mrs. H," Sorcha protested.

"Did she tell you anything, Mrs. H? Why is she so sad?" Mary asked in a quivering voice.

Paul knew he shouldn't be listening to their conversation, but they seemed to have forgotten he was at the table. He kept his coffee cup in his hand, despite it being empty. He didn't want to move in case they noticed him.

"She told me nothing and she won't tell you anything either if you keep at her. She needs some peace and quiet. Miss Sorcha, you best ask Miss Emer to call out to see her. She might need to bring the doctor, too."

"The doctor?" Both women responded as Paul jumped up.

"What's wrong with Miss Murphy?"

The women registered him with a look before switching their attention back to Mrs. H.

"Miss Laura was shot. I've seen enough bullet wounds to recognize one when I see it. It looks clean to me, but I would feel better if Miss Emer or Doc examined her."

"Shot?" Sorcha and Mary exchanged glances before turning back to Mrs. H.

"I'll go now and bring the doc back with me." Paul put his coffee cup on the table. "Excuse me, ladies."

"There is no rush, Paul. She's sleeping now and she needs rest more than anything. You have another piece of pie and then you can go home. My Aaron is going into town later. He can ask the doc to call out."

Paul sat back down, but he didn't take any more pie. He couldn't stomach it. Who would shoot a woman, especially one who looked as beautiful as Miss Murphy?

"Poor Laura. Why didn't I write to her sooner and get her to come to Clover Springs?" Mary stood up, wringing her hands.

"Sit down, Mary. Laura wouldn't have come. You

know she thought we were crazy to become mail order brides. Whatever happened to Laura wasn't your fault," Sorcha said in a comforting tone.

"But she's our friend. We should have done something," Mary said, her voice quivering as her eyes filled with tears.

"You can't change the past, Miss Mary. No point in crying tears over what's happened. Today is the only day that matters. We don't know what the future brings, so no point in worrying about anything other than today." Mrs. H started banging pots around. "Miss Laura needs sleep and nourishment. I'm going to make her some chicken soup. That will help put meat on her bones. She's too skinny. Looks like she hasn't eaten properly in a long time."

Sorcha stood up. "I best get back, too. Nandita is due to bring Meggie and Jenny back later today. She said she'd bring dinner, too, but I might make some apple pies."

"I will drop you home, Mrs. Petersen." Paul stood up again. "Thank you for the pie, Mrs. H."

"Mary, I will call back tomorrow. Tell Laura I said goodbye." Sorcha picked up her shawl. "Thank you, Mrs. H. You are exactly what Laura needs."

CHAPTER 17

Laura lay on the bed trying to muster the courage to get dressed and go downstairs. She knew Mary wouldn't be happy unless she was told every detail, but she couldn't talk about it now. Maybe not ever. A knock on the door caused her stomach to turn over. She sat up, staring at the door.

Her shoulders sagged with relief and she sank back onto the bed as Mrs. H walked in.

"Good evening, Miss Laura. Are you decent? The doc came to check you. Miss Emer wasn't available."

Laura snuggled further under the covers. She didn't want a man touching her, even if he was a doctor. The door opened, admitting the housekeeper and an old, grey-haired gentleman with a handlebar moustache and a long beard.

"Would you like me to stay with you, Miss Laura, while the doc examines you?"

"I'm fine, Mrs. H. I don't need to see anyone."

"You may think you are fine, but I won't be happy until I check you out, young lady. Mrs. H tells me you've been shot. I'd like to check the wound, please." The doctor had a kind voice, but Laura still looked to Mrs. H for help.

Mrs. H smiled reassuringly, but Laura couldn't smile back. She didn't want anyone else examining her. The doctor would have questions.

"Miss Laura, stop looking so nervous. The doc is a kind old man. He isn't going to poke around in your business. He's just going to check that wound. You can trust him, okay?"

"Of course you can trust me. Now, let me see the wound. There's a good girl." The doctor ahhed and ummed over the wound, making Laura move her arm this way and that. "No swelling and the wound itself looks clean. Whoever looked after you did a fine job, Miss Murphy. You still need to rest the arm, but you should recover fully in time."

Laura waited for the questions, but none came. The doctor rinsed his hands in the bowl and picked up his bag.

"Thank you. Doctor, I have a little money. Mrs. H, could you get my bag please?"

"My bill has been paid, Miss Murphy. You rest a while and then you need to start exercising the arm. Gently at first, don't try carrying any heavy pots just yet."

The doctor looked at her steadily for a couple of seconds. "I noticed the bruising and other marks."

Laura's cheeks grew warm as she looked away. The doctor continued talking, his voice gentle.

"If you want a more thorough examination, you come to my office in town. You don't have to tell me anything about you or how you came to be shot, but if you ever need my services, please don't be afraid. There is nothing you can tell me that would shock these old ears." With that, he patted the bed and walked out the door, leaving Laura staring after him. Was everyone in Clover Springs so nice and accommodating?

CHAPTER 18

Laura concentrated on standing up. Her legs were shaking and she didn't want to fall back onto the bed.

"Is anyone else here?"

"Only Miss Mary and Cathy."

"Who is Cathy?"

"Miss Mary's baby. Didn't you know she had a little girl? She is the cutest little thing you ever saw." Mrs. H bustled around the room. "Now, do you want some help getting dressed?"

Laura didn't answer the somewhat rhetorical question, given Mrs. H had already started helping her. It was nice to be looked after by someone who didn't seem to want anything back in return. She enjoyed having her hair brushed; it was a totally new feeling to be so relaxed in someone else's company.

"Did you like your soup? You have to eat more or your bones will continue to poke out. Miss Mary can afford it, you know. There isn't any shortage of food here. She told me what it was like for you girls in the orphanage."

"The soup was lovely, thank you. I was just too tired to eat much."

"Well, I hope you are hungry now. I got bacon and eggs and some biscuits waiting downstairs."

Laura wasn't hungry, but she didn't want to disappoint the woman who had been so kind to her. She agreed to eat a little. Mrs. H chattered the whole way down the stairs and into the kitchen. There, they found Mary sitting at the table with Cathy.

"She's beautiful, Mary." Laura tried her best to keep her tone positive. Seeing the baby brought back memories of her own loss. She held a hand over her stomach. Johnny had lost at cards that night, too. His punishment had ended in her losing their first child. He'd been happy she wasn't pregnant any longer. *Having children with you isn't part of my plan.* She shivered. His voice, inside her head, was so loud it was as if he were in the room with her.

"Thank you, Laura. You look much better already." Mary's concerned eyes showed she was lying, but Laura knew her friend was just trying to make her feel at home. "Mrs. H has cooked up a huge breakfast."

Laura sat at the table.

"Would you like to hold Cathy?"

"Maybe later," Laura replied, hardening her heart to the look on Mary's face. She had to protect herself. She wasn't ready to hold a baby, especially one as gorgeous as this little one.

She wasn't going to stay in Clover Springs and didn't want to make any attachments. Although she had slept better last night because she felt safe and secure, she knew it wouldn't last. The women would want to know her story, and once they did, she'd be sent away. It was best she leave first.

Desperate to change the subject, she thanked the housekeeper. "Thank you, Mrs. H. It looks like a feast."

Laura stared at the heaping plate in front of her, thinking of how many children the food in front of her would feed. As if reading her mind, Mary spoke.

"I was the same when I first arrived. I couldn't believe the amount of food Mrs. H prepared for every meal. The men work hard and need their energy. You need it, too, Laura. I, on the other hand, could do with losing a few pounds."

"Don't you start that again, Miss Mary. You are feeding your baby and need all the nourishment I can provide."

"Yes, Ma!" Mary quipped, making Laura smile. These two women enjoyed a special relationship.

Something she'd never had. She couldn't understand why, but with women, her relationships always followed the same pattern. They either shunned her or made fun of her. Nobody, apart from Wilma, just wanted to be her friend. Mary and Sorcha did. *Yes, and then they left too.*

Not liking the direction her thoughts were taking, she picked up a fork to start eating. Then she heard noises outside. The door opened and suddenly the room was full of men. Laura tried her best to shrink into the seat, hoping against hope nobody would notice her.

"Laura, this is Davy, my husband. The other men are Mrs. H's boys, Aaron and Samuel. You remember Paul Kelley. He drove you from the station."

Laura forced a smile as she greeted the men.

"Sit down, boys, and eat up before breakfast gets cold. The coffee is strong, just how you like it." Mrs. H smiled at each of the men as she laid a plate full of food in front of them.

Laura played with the food on her plate as the conversation went on around her. She could see everyone got on very well together. There were no awkward silences. If the men noticed she wasn't talking, they didn't comment. Only after they had finished eating and were ready to leave did they speak to her directly.

"Nice to meet you, Ma'am. Mary told me a lot about you," Davy said before smiling over at his wife.

The room swam as she struggled to get out of her seat. She tried to breathe, but couldn't. Her heart was beating too fast, making her feel dizzy.

"Sit down, Miss Laura. You've gone a funny color. Drink some water." Paul held her elbow as he guided her back into the seat. The other men disappeared from the room as Mrs. H ushered everyone out the door. She could hear Cathy fussing on Mary's lap, but she couldn't seem to focus her eyes.

"You feeling a little better?" the low velvety voice asked.

Laura moaned with shame. *What must they think of me?*

"I'm so sorry. I don't know what to say."

"Just sit and drink your water. You have nothing to be sorry for," Paul said.

He was still holding her arm, but she didn't mind. He wasn't a bit like Johnny. He had a serene gentleness about him. Instinctively she thought he wouldn't hurt anyone, but she had been wrong about men before. She pulled her arm away from him, ignoring his reaction. If he had any ideas about her, he best get rid of them now. There was no future for her with any man. Not now, not ever.

Paul didn't comment on the fact that she had taken

her arm away. He was too angry at the man or men who had caused her to react so violently to a simple statement. Davy Sullivan wouldn't hurt a fly. But this lady wasn't to know that. The feeling that she had suffered a great deal grew.

"I should be getting back to work."

"Yes, of course. Please don't let me keep you. I'm fine now. Just overtired from the journey."

Her hair fell across her eyes as she muttered her apology. He resisted the urge to push it back. Not only would it be inappropriate for him to touch her, but given her fragile state, he would probably scare her.

"Why don't you go back to bed, Miss Murphy? It's a long journey from Boston and the seats on the train are so hard. They make your…" Embarrassed at where the conversation was going, Paul took a deep breath. "What I meant to say was the air here in Clover Springs is cleaner. Most people say they feel really tired the first few days."

Laura stared up at him, assessing him quietly, although her eyes showed a hint of amusement. He stared back, not flinching from her gaze. A small smile played around her lips, but then it was gone.

He couldn't wait for the day when her whole face lit up from smiling. He was going to do everything in his power to make that happen. He didn't know what it would take. It would be a challenge, but one he was going to enjoy.

Time to go. "Enjoy the rest of your day, Miss Murphy."

"Thank you, Mr. Kelley."

CHAPTER 19

Paul threw the blankets back. It was pointless trying to sleep. His mind was too busy. Dressing quickly, he decided to do some work in the barn. In his spare time, he liked to work with wood. His pa had started him whittling little pieces when he was a boy. He always said he had a gift for seeing something in a piece of wood. Working with his hands helped him to relax.

He loved animals, but rearing cattle wasn't in his blood. He hated plowing and the other chores associated with farming. If he could, he would spend all his time making things. There was money to be made, since the more successful ranchers or miners either didn't have time or the knowledge to make things for themselves, but he was tied to the farm. He told his ma the extra cash Davy paid him for doing jobs around the Sullivan ranch came in useful. And it did. But the reality was, it gave him an excuse to do what he loved doing. Working with his hands, making things.

He'd been dreaming his older brother had come back, leaving him free to become a carpenter and to marry Laura. Ma could live with Jackson and his wife. But then he'd woken up. Jackson would never come back to Colorado, but even if he did, his wife would kill Ma rather than live with her. He could understand why; the woman would drive a… He smelt coffee. Ma was up.

"There you are. I thought you would have started early on the chores. The farm doesn't run itself, you know."

"It's still early, Ma. I'm going out to the barn to work on some of the furniture Mary Sullivan asked me to make." He'd made a bed for Davy Sullivan and Mary had asked if he could make a small table to match.

"That man spoils that wife of his."

"Davy is generous, Ma, but he can afford to be. It helps me, too. You know I love working with my hands."

"You wouldn't need to be making furniture for other couples if you married Ida Hawthorn. It's time you settled down and raised a family. Time is moving on."

"Ma, stop it. I'm not marrying Miss Hawthorn. I know who I want."

"It better not be that girl who arrived at the Sullivan's last week. Why does a pretty girl always turn a man's head? She is no more fit to run this farm than I am to do a jig."

"Ma, you don't know anything about Miss Murphy."

"I know she's another one of those orphans from Boston. She's got a questionable past. She's wearing a wedding ring but no sign of a husband. She may be wearing a black dress, but it's hardly widow weeds from what I heard."

"Ma, this isn't the Civil War years. Women don't go into deep mourning anymore. Times have changed."

"They haven't changed that much, son. Doc had to see her the first day she arrived here. Rumor has it that she's with child. Probably isn't even married, knowing her sort."

Paul stared at his ma. How on earth did she learn so much when she hadn't left the farm in years? *Ida Hawthorn.* He'd seen her huddled with Mrs. Shaw in town a couple of days ago. They must have been gossiping about Laura.

"Don't make judgments about people you haven't met, Ma. Laura Murphy is a widow and deserves our compassion. Remember what the Good Book says."

"Don't be cheeky, boy. I know my Bible. I also know you, and your head's been turned by that girl. If she's a widow, why are you calling her Miss Murphy?"

Paul had no answer to that. Sorcha had introduced her as Laura Murphy, and he just assumed she wasn't married. He'd been calling her Miss Murphy since. Nobody corrected him, either. But she was wearing a wedding ring and her dress had been black. He wasn't sure of her story, but he wasn't about to argue with his ma. She wouldn't listen. She was still talking.

"Before she arrived, you were happy to marry Ida. Now you walk around with your head in the clouds. The Sullivan guest is no match for you, Paul Kelley. The sooner you accept that, the better."

Paul walked away, leaving his mother talking to herself. He couldn't help thinking about Laura. She was the reason he couldn't sleep. He found himself making excuses to go visit the Sullivans just to catch a glimpse of her. She was still as nervous as a filly, but he hoped over time she would see he meant her no harm.

Was it true? Was she too good for him? He didn't have much and he wasn't as handsome as some of the men in town. Maybe she had set her heart on someone else already.

CHAPTER 20

Laura opened the kitchen door, about to step outside to get some air. Instead, she found herself staring into Paul Kelley's eyes. She'd promised there would be no more men in her life, yet here she was eagerly anticipating Paul's visit. He was so attractive. His wavy brown hair curled at the collar of his shirt. Would it feel as soft as it looked, if she ran her fingers through it? *Get a hold of yourself.*

"Morning, Miss Murphy. You're up early. Are you heading into town?"

His voice made her insides melt; she could listen to him speak all day. Her brain refused to engage.

"Do you want breakfast, boys? What you doing standing in the doorway? Are you going to stand there all day, Miss Laura?"

Jerked from her daydreaming by Mrs. Higgins

question, Laura stood back to let the men go through to the kitchen. She stared after them.

"Admiring the view?" Mary asked, her eyes teasing.

"Yes. Isn't it wonderful? The mountains are so majestic." Laura knew she wasn't fooling Mary, but she wasn't about to admit to finding Paul Kelley fascinating.

"I thought it was something entirely different that caught your attention. Or should I say *someone*."

"Not at all. I was lost in thought. I have to make a decision on what I am going to do."

"What do you mean?"

"Mary, I have to get a job. I can't live on your charity forever. The last week or so has been lovely, but it's time to make a change. My arm is better now."

"Laura, forget about getting a job. You have to get married again. Clover Springs is a nice town, but it's no place for a single woman. Being married will give you respectability as well as protection."

"Nobody will want to marry me, Mary. I'm ruined." Laura dug her nails into the palms of her hands. She wasn't going to cry anymore. It was pointless.

"What do you mean ruined? You are a widow. That's respectable." Mary didn't give Laura a chance to reply. "Laura, there are lots of men who would marry you. You are beautiful, not to mention hardworking.

This isn't Boston. There aren't enough women out here for men to get picky.

"Oh good, someone will marry me because they are desperate."

"Stop it, Laura, I didn't mean it like that and you know it. I wouldn't hurt you on purpose. Father Molloy sent you here to get married. He must have thought that best."

"He knew I couldn't stay in Boston."

"Why?"

Laura stared at Mary. It was time to tell her the truth. She had evaded her questions for long enough. Although, to be fair, Mary hadn't pressed her for answers. Perhaps she had sensed Laura's need to get her thoughts straight first.

"Walk with me. I'll tell you my story, but I don't want anyone to overhear us. Mrs. H knows some of it."

"You told Mrs. H and not us?"

She cringed inside at the hurt in Mary's voice, but how could she explain the older woman had caught her at a weak moment? She had poured her heart out to her after the woman had helped her dress for bed one night. Mrs. H had brushed her hair without comment as Laura had sobbed her way through the horror of the last couple of years. She didn't regret telling the housekeeper, but she was sorry she had hurt Mary in the process.

She sent Mary a look pleading for understanding before she started walking.

"Johnny, my husband, wasn't a good man. I didn't know it at first, but he was involved in gambling. He wasn't respectable. He owned a saloon." Laura watched Mary's face to see her reaction.

At the look of shock on Mary's face, Laura crossed her arms around her chest. "He had girls there. You know, the ones who entertained customers. I didn't do that. The only man I slept with was Johnny. He kept threatening to sell me to customers, but he never did. It was just one of the many ways he used to make me do whatever he wanted."

"Laura, I am so sorry." Tears flowed unchecked down Mary's face. Laura couldn't stand being the reason her friend was hurting—but she had to know the truth. It was the only way she would forget about matchmaking.

"Why didn't you go to Father Molloy for help?

Laura shrugged her shoulders.

"That's not the worst of it. When he died, there was a large amount of gold in his safe. More than he could win at cards. I don't know where it came from. The police didn't believe me at first, but Father Molloy convinced them. Seems some of the working girls told them Johnny had connections all over Boston and elsewhere.

"How did Johnny die?"

"He used to cheat at cards. He married me because of my gift." She saw Mary flinch at her sarcastic reference to her perfect memory.

"What has your gift got to do with cards?"

"He knew I could memorize the pack of cards and know the odds of the next card. He trained me in every game they played at the saloon. When he was playing for a big stake, he made me dress up. The gowns he picked didn't leave much covered. He said between my body and my memory, the other guys hadn't had a chance."

"What a vile man. I'm glad he's dead. If he wasn't, I would want to strangle him." Mary's cheeks flushed as her temper got the better of her.

"He's dead all right. His luck ran out. At that last game, the men he was playing with guessed he was cheating. They shot him. It was all my fault, too."

"That's how you got hurt?"

"The bullet went through him and into my shoulder. I could say he died in my arms, but I don't remember. I passed out." Laura sniffed, eyeing the tears running down Mary's face. "I woke up in the hospital. Father Molloy found me there, and now I am here."

"Why would him getting shot be your fault? You didn't shoot him, Laura."

"No, but I wished he was dead. The evening he died, I got distracted. A man, a poor man, had won at one of the tables. You should have seen the men desperate enough to think they could change their lives by winning money. I lost count of how many men I saw lose." Laura swallowed the lump in her throat. She had to tell Mary now or she would never do it. "Johnny would let a man win a couple of games. Then, just when the man thought he was on a winning streak and couldn't lose, Johnny's staff would arrange it so he lost."

Laura hesitated as she tried to deal with the terror generated by remembering that last night in the saloon.

"This one man had won quite a lot of money. I was urging him to leave before he tried his hand at another table and lost. I wasn't paying attention to Johnny's table. I lost track of the cards." Laura gulped, trying to quell the fear the memory triggered. "Johnny wasn't happy. I knew he would punish me later. I prayed something would happen so I wouldn't get hurt. He died."

"He died because he cheated and got caught. That has nothing to do with you. You don't have the power of life and death, Laura."

They came to a little bench. "Sit down, Laura. Davy

put this bench here for me to rest when I was pregnant with Cathy. It has the nicest view."

Both women sat. Mary took Laura's hand and held it in hers.

"You know what the nuns would say. They held me responsible for Widow Murphy dying shortly after she found me. They said I was cursed, and they were right."

Laura pulled her hand away from Mary. She buried her head in her hands and sobbed. Mary put her arm around her, but she shook it off. She didn't want to taint anyone with the evil that grew inside her.

"You are no more cursed than I am. Sure, you have an unusual gift, but it is the same as Katie being blessed with the ability to sew beautifully. There is a reason God gave you a perfect memory, and it certainly wasn't to help the likes of this Johnny at cards." Mary wiped her eyes with a handkerchief. "The nuns said a lot of things to all of us, Laura. We have to do our best to forget the bad stuff and concentrate on the good. Do you remember Sister Una used to say how special you were? You have to believe that. You are also loved."

Mary sat quietly for a few minutes. Laura tried to compose herself, but the next question voiced the biggest fear she had.

"Does Father Molloy think these friends of Johnny's are going to try to find you?"

Laura gave a little nod but stayed silent. In her dreams, men came after her, but she didn't know who most of them were. They didn't have faces. Except for one. Coleman. His face stayed with her all the time, whether she was asleep or not.

"This is serious, Laura. We have to tell the sheriff. He'll know what to do."

"I'm not staying in Clover Springs. If the men come after me, who knows what they will do? I can't risk you, Sorcha or any of your friends being hurt on my account. I shouldn't have come here in the first place. I need to go."

"Where?"

"I don't know. California, maybe. Somewhere nobody knows me."

"You can't go alone. I won't let you, and neither will the girls. Laura, you are like a sister to us. We all know what the orphanage was like. You and Sorcha had the worst of it there, but those shared experiences are what make us like family. I am closer to you girls than I am to my sister, Cathy.

"Where is Cathy now?"

"Somewhere in Europe. I barely get one letter a year from her. Don't go. Stay here. Marry and settle in

Clover Springs. You have friends, Laura. We will help you."

"No, Mary, I can't bring trouble to your door."

"Who says you will? For all you know the men in Boston don't even know about you. I don't think a man is going to credit a woman for his luck at cards, do you?"

"The girls in the saloon knew. They hated me. In their eyes, Johnny treated me better than them. He gave me nicer clothes and he didn't make me see any other men."

"You were his wife."

"Maybe."

"What? I thought you said you were married."

"I did. I thought we were, but the police said Johnny's name wasn't really Johnny. He wasn't from Boston but from New York. He could have a wife already. In fact, he could have several."

Laura fought to keep control, not liking the sound of hysteria in her voice. She dug the nails harder into her palms to distract herself from the panic threatening to overwhelm her. It had been one thing living with the knowledge she had married a gambler and a thief. It was another to have lived in sin with him.

"You are not leaving Clover Springs. Now you are here; we are all together again. You, me, Katie, Sorcha, and of course Emer. We are family, whether you like it or not. So I don't want to hear another word about you going to California or anywhere else. Family sticks together."

Laura couldn't believe her ears. Mary knew the whole story, yet she still wanted her to stay. She hadn't thrown her out. What about the others, would they feel the same way?

"Yes, Sorcha and Katie will agree with me. Emer will likely shoot you herself if you try to leave."

"How did you know I was thinking about them?"

Mary wrapped her arm around the younger girl's shoulders. "I told you. We are family and it's only natural you would care what they think. Just so you know, they love you as much as I do."

"Emer doesn't know me. She's a nurse and respectable." Laura wanted to believe Mary, but her negative experiences with other people made it difficult.

"Sorcha and I are respectable married women now." Mary smiled, letting Laura know she was teasing. Then her face grew as serious as her tone. "Emer would be the last person to judge anyone. She's a nurse now, but once she lived with outlaws. She can shoot straighter than most men. She doesn't know you, but she loves Sorcha and Sorcha loves you. So Emer would make sure you stay here."

Laura bit her knuckle, making Mary swipe it out of her mouth.

"I thought you gave up that disgusting habit years ago. It's worse than biting your nails." Mary stood up. "Now come on. Mrs. H was baking earlier. I'm starving."

"Thank you, Mary."

Laura let Mary put her arms around her and pull her into a hug. "We love you, Laura. Stay in Clover Springs and let our children be as good friends as we are."

Laura stiffened, causing Mary to push her back gently.

"What's wrong now?"

"I'm never going to have children. Nobody will want to marry me, especially when they know the full story."

"Nobody has to know everything, Laura. It's up to you who you tell. I won't say a word. As to nobody wanting to marry you, I think you have forgotten a certain cowboy. I swear I haven't seen Paul Kelley as much in the last four years as I have seen him over the last week."

Laura's cheeks glowed, causing Mary to look at her speculatively.

"If I am not mistaken, I don't think you are as immune to his charms as you claim, either."

Laura opened her mouth, but Mary put her finger against it. "Don't bother denying it. I've seen how you look at him when you think nobody is looking. He's a fine man, as Mrs. H would say." Mary linked Laura's arm and half pulled her along as they walked toward the house. "We'll go into town tomorrow and see the sheriff. He'll tell us what to do."

CHAPTER 21

Mary insisted Laura take a nap that afternoon. She was worn out from telling her story, and Mary didn't want her to lapse back into melancholy. Davy was going to town, so Mary decided to go with him. She wanted to talk to Katie.

Sorcha and Emer had made plans to have lunch every Wednesday, so she knew she would catch up with them, too. Mrs. H almost jumped for joy at the chance to spend some time alone with Cathy.

"You all right, Mary? You are awfully quiet." Davy stroked her arm with one hand, driving the wagon with the other.

"Laura told me her story. It didn't make for easy listening, but I'm glad she came to live here. That orphanage has a lot to answer for," Mary said, seething as the image of Mother Superior came to mind.

Davy kissed her lightly on the top of her head. "I am very thankful to it. You wouldn't be here if it wasn't for the nuns."

"True. They did do *some* good."

"Nothing's ever black and white, darling. We've learnt that the hard way."

Mary stared up at her husband's profile. She loved him more with every passing day. He had given her everything she wanted, and not just material things, which were lovely. More importantly, he gave her a family of her own. He loved her and trusted her completely. He had made huge efforts to control his jealousy and, for the most part, he'd been successful. She'd fallen deeper in love with him when he'd brought Ben to live in Clover Springs, and now they were parents to Cathy, too. Their lives couldn't get much better.

Mrs. H. In all the drama surrounding Laura's arrival, she'd forgotten their housekeeper had troubles. How could she have done that?

"Davy, we have to find a way of keeping Aaron and Samuel in Clover Springs."

"What can we do? You know I don't hold with telling other people how to live their lives, darling."

"Yes, but if they leave, Mrs. H will be brokenhearted. She said she's too old to go with them. Can we not try to find a way to keep them here?"

Davy glanced down at her before switching his attention back to the horses. "What did you have in mind? They said they want to go mining for gold. Not much chance of finding gold in Clover Springs."

"I don't think they are that keen on going mining. Not after Harry's chat with them the other night."

"Did you have something to do with that, Mary?"

Mary smiled up at him. "I may have had a chat with Elizabeth."

Davy grunted.

"Lizzie said her blood still rushes to her head if she thinks about the risks Harry took working in the mines."

Harry, Davy's brother-in-law, had spent three years in the mines high up in the mountains before marrying his sister Elizabeth. Mary had told Lizzie about Mrs. Higgins being upset, so Lizzie asked him to speak to the boys.

"I don't remember his stories being quite so gory before."

"Lizzie may have asked him to labor that point a little. Don't look at me like that, Davy. Mrs. H has been so kind to me and to our family. I can't bear the thought of her being brokenhearted. Mining is dangerous. You hear about accidents in the coal mines every day."

"The boys aren't interested in coal mining."

Davy held his hand up at the look she gave him. "Okay, I get your point. So do you have any ideas on how to get the boys to stay here?"

"I thought you and Lawrence might be able to help them file a claim under the Homestead Act." She eyed Davy's thoughtful expression. "I don't know much about it, except you have to live on the land for five years, you have to build a house, and probably a hundred other things."

"It's not that bad. The boys would have to go to Denver and file a claim with the Land Office. That costs ten dollars, plus there is a commission of two dollars on top."

"That's not too bad, is it? Would the boys have that type of money?"

"They need more than that, Mary. What are they going to use the land for? If they are going to farm it, they will need money for crops and tools, not to mention the cost of building a small house. They are experienced ranch hands; they may want to raise cattle."

"But you could give them some of ours. We have loads."

Davy laughed before giving her a squeeze. "I love

how generous you are, but the boys might not feel the same way. Charity is a hard thing to swallow."

"It's not charity." As Davy arched his eyebrows, Mary continued quickly. "We could make it a wedding present."

"So you are going to turn the boys into homesteaders and husbands all in one go?"

Mary's cheeks flamed at the teasing tone.

"Have you found the boys wives already, or do they get to pick those themselves?"

"I thought about writing to Mrs. Gantley."

"Who?"

"Mrs. Gantley. She's the lady who helped Katie get here."

"The woman who matched her to a train robber."

"Davy." Mary playfully punched her husband. "You know she didn't do that on purpose, and if Katie hadn't been on the train…"

"Okay, so you want to send for wives for the Higgins boys. Without telling them?"

Mary couldn't return his look, but found something of interest on the horizon. "I thought it best not to. They would only insist on going to California."

"I don't like it, Mary. It's one thing trying to talk them out of going mining by making Harry tell his stories. But getting them wives? What about the women who come here hoping to find love and happiness? Not really fair to them either, is it?"

Disappointed and a little ashamed, Mary slumped back in the wagon seat. She hadn't thought it through.

"What about asking the boys? They may agree to writing to the bride woman."

"Doubt it. They will say they can't afford to support a wife and family. Mrs. H said the reason they were going to California was because they want to build something of their own." Mary swallowed hard. She didn't want to push her husband too far, but at the same time she felt she owed it to Mrs. H to try her best. "I thought you might encourage the boys to talk to Lawrence. With the mining boom there is a demand for beef, or if they prefer farming, for food."

Davy nodded but didn't say anything. Mary waited a couple of seconds, but her lack of patience got the better of her.

"Would you talk to them, Davy? They'd listen to you."

Davy remained silent. Mary knew he was considering the idea, but he would think about it for a while. He wasn't one for making quick decisions, which was something she had learnt to be more patient about.

"Think about it, that's all I am asking." Mary kissed her husband's cheek as they arrived at the store.

"There's Katie. Don't worry about collecting me. I will walk home. Might help me shift some of this baby fat."

She squealed as Davy put his arms around her, bringing her up against his chest. "I like your curves, Mrs. Sullivan." He kissed her thoroughly, leaving her breathless and red-faced. "Enjoy your visit. Don't do anything about Mrs. Gantley and the wives just yet. You hear?"

Mary nodded. She couldn't speak as she tried to get her breath back after his embrace.

* * *

"POOR LAURA, no wonder she's looked so miserable. If I got my hands on that man, I would shoot him," Emer said angrily.

"I told Laura you would." Mary smiled at Emer.

"I'm glad Father Molloy sent her here to us. The sheriff will know what to do. Do you want me to come with you, Mary?"

"No, but thanks, Katie. I don't want the man thinking he is being besieged."

The women laughed. The sheriff was a self-proclaimed bachelor. He often said he didn't have time for emotional women. The last thing he'd want would be a group of them turning up at the jailhouse tomorrow.

* * *

LAURA WAS PACING the floor when Mary returned home.

"Did you see the sheriff? What did he say?" she asked, wringing her hands together.

"Calm down, Laura."

Laura allowed Mary to lead her to the rocking chairs set out on the porch. "Sit down and take a deep breath. I didn't see the sheriff. I went into town to speak to Katie and the others. They agreed with me. You need to let the sheriff know trouble may come to Clover Springs. It is not just for your own protection. These friends of your husband may hurt someone in town. You can't take that risk."

Laura stared into Mary's face. She wasn't sure she was brave enough to tell a stranger her story.

"Laura, trust me. It's for the best. Katie and Emer agree with me. You have to do this."

Laura took a deep breath. Mary was right. She had to do this, if only to help protect her friends should Coleman decide to pursue her.

"Yes, Mary. I'll go tomorrow. But…could you come with me please?"

"Of course I will." Mary hugged her close. "Just try and stop me."

CHAPTER 22

Laura's head hurt. She hadn't been able to sleep. She lost count of how many times she wished she'd never told Mary the full truth. She should have known her friend would seek help from the law. She didn't bother trying to eat anything for breakfast. The smells wafting up from the kitchen were enough for her stomach to roil. She ran back to her room and splashed cold water on her face. *Stop being a coward. You have to do this.*

She walked down the stairs slowly. Mary stood waiting, her concern evident by the look on her face. She smiled but Laura was unable to smile back. Her face was frozen.

"I know you are scared but you can do this. You have survived worse. I am so proud of you, Laura Murphy."

Mary squeezed her hand as she spoke. While grateful for the sentiment, Laura didn't feel brave. She wanted to run away, to go somewhere nobody knew her. But it was too late for that now.

Davy drove the wagon into town with Mary and Laura sitting beside him. Mrs. H had agreed to look after Cathy. They tied the wagon outside the store. Davy had business in town. He offered to accompany Mary and Laura, but they declined. Holding hands, they walked through town.

The jailhouse wasn't busy. Laura found herself concentrating on the wanted posters while Mary filled the sheriff in on why they were here. She was so glad Mary was here with her. Her stomach churned as she waited to hear what the lawman thought.

"You orphans sure like to keep me busy, Miss Mary."

"I told you I should leave town, Mary." Laura took a step toward the door, but the sheriff moved to stand in front of her.

"You should stay in Clover Springs, young lady. Pretty thing like you shouldn't be alone. I am glad you had the sense to call yourself by your old name. Less likely your husband's friends will find you." The sheriff paused as if to spit out the tobacco he'd been chewing. Looking at the two women, he pushed it to the side of his mouth. "You have good friends here in town. Misses Emer, Sorcha, Katie and Miss Mary here are some of the best people to ever land in Colorado State."

"But Sheriff, you said we bring trouble. That certainly could be the case with me. Mr. Coleman made some threats. I have no idea whether Johnny has other enemies who will want to track me down."

"I didn't say the trouble you orphans bring isn't welcome. It helps keep life interesting. Miss Emer couldn't help the fact the Bainstreet Gang came here. The same goes for you. You are not responsible for your husband's actions, Miss Murphy. Plain and simple."

"Thank you, Sheriff."

"Now, you may not be thanking me in a minute. You best get married as soon as you can, Miss Murphy. You don't want to be found alone by the type of men your husband was involved with."

At Laura's gasp, the sheriff added, "this Coleman has a bad reputation; I've heard of him. He is not a gentleman, and I wouldn't trust him with a full grown rattlesnake, never mind a pretty lady like you." The sheriff put his hands in his suspenders. "Nope. A single woman needs protection."

"But wouldn't getting married put my husband at risk? I should go away," Laura said, but her reluctance to leave was obvious in her tone.

"Getting married means you could stay in Clover Springs. Nobody needs to know about your previous connections. You came from Boston just like the other mail order brides."

"Listen to the sheriff. He's been doing this job a long time. He knows how men like them operate."

"Less of the doing the job a long time, Miss Mary. Anyone would think you thought I was old."

The three of them laughed. Laura guessed that was the sheriff's intention. He seemed like a kind man, tough but fair. Emer had told her about how he had released her into the custody of the town doctor when trouble had followed her to Clover Springs last year.

She knew she was frowning again. She didn't want to get married. She couldn't bear the thought of being intimate with anyone. She shivered with revulsion. Johnny had seemed so kind and thoughtful at first. Look how wrong she had been about him.

"I'll think about what you said, Sheriff. Come on, Mary, let's go see Katie."

"Don't spend too long thinking, Miss Murphy. Trouble has a way of not waiting for any man. Or woman." The sheriff sat back down behind his desk, stroking his tobacco stained beard. Laura didn't say anything but left with Mary following behind her.

"Good morning, Miss Murphy, Mrs. Sullivan."

The last man Laura wanted to see now was

standing in front of them. Paul smiled, but his smile dropped when they stared. "Are you ladies in trouble? Couldn't help but notice you coming out of the jail-house. Miss Emer isn't locked up again, is she?"

His attempt at a joke also fell flat. Laura could see Mary looking from her to Paul and back again. Her friend was waiting for her to say something, but she didn't know what. *Oh yes, Paul, we were just telling the sheriff how it's all my fault my husband was murdered.*

"Laura has to get married and was just asking the sheriff to give her away."

Both Paul and Laura stared at Mary, who colored prettily as she fidgeted with a thread on her skirt.

"Married, you? You're getting hitched. Already? To who?" Paul seemed to realize he was firing words at her. He pulled at the collar of his shirt. "Excuse my manners. What I meant to ask was, who is the lucky man?"

Laura opened her mouth, but no words came out. Mary rushed to the rescue once more. "She hasn't decided yet."

Laura could have groaned out loud. The look of confusion, and even hope on Paul's face, would have been amusing had it been any other time. Now she was simply mortified. She sounded like a harlot. A desperate woman who'd settle for any man. *Well, aren't you?*

"What Mary is trying to say, Mr. Kelley, is, well, it's a little embarrassing. I don't know quite how to explain."

"Laura came to Clover Springs to get married. She knew we were mail order brides, and she assumed we would be able to find her a groom. And we would, wouldn't we, Mr. Kelley?"

This time Laura did groan. Aloud. *The poor man. He must think I planned this from the start. Mary has just about asked him to take my hand in marriage.*

"Please excuse us, Mr. Kelley. Mary was up late with the baby and she isn't thinking straight. Her mouth always did move faster than her brain. Isn't that right, Mary?"

When Mary failed to answer, Laura gave her a slight kick. Mary recovered quickly. "Cathy, darling as she is, must be teething. I'm worn out. Good day, Mr. Kelley. I hope we see you soon."

Mary had to shout the last bit as Laura pulled her down the street, leaving Paul Kelley standing in the middle of the road staring after them

So she had come to Clover Springs to get married and she wasn't courting anyone yet. If he had understood Mrs. Sullivan, there was a good chance she saw

him as a potential groom. Paul had to restrain himself from dancing down the street. Miss Murphy might agree to marry him. Ma won't like it. Ma can go to…

"What's put that silly grin on your face?"

Paul looked up to see Davy Sullivan smiling down at him, his expression slightly wary. *He probably thinks I'm drunk.*

"Your wife." At the glare Davy sent his direction, he gave himself a quick kick. "What I meant was Miss Mary just about told me to start courting Miss Murphy. Isn't she the finest woman you ever laid eyes on?"

"Are you talking about Miss Murphy or my wife, Kelley?"

"Miss Murphy, of course."

"I think the sun has got to you, Kelley. You need a cold shower. Maybe a chat with your ma. She's never going to agree to you marrying an orphan."

Paul didn't care about his ma. He wanted to confirm he had understood the conversation. He walked quickly to the doctor's office, relieved to find Emer alone. He didn't relish explaining to Mrs. Grey he wasn't sure if the lady he liked, loved even, wanted to get married.

"Is it true, Miss Emer? Did Miss Murphy come here to find a husband?"

Emer stared at him for such a long time, he

thought he had made a total fool of himself. "I'm sorry, Miss Emer. I just met Miss Murphy coming out of the sheriff's office. Mrs. Sullivan was with her and she said something about needing to get married. Miss Murphy, not Mrs. Sullivan. Oh, I am making a mess of this."

"Sit down, Paul. When Laura came here, we thought she wanted to get married. Now, well, I don't know what to tell you. It's not my story to tell, but Miss Murphy has her reasons for wanting to stay single."

"Was it because she was shot? You know I would never hurt a lady, Miss Emer."

"I know, Paul, but it isn't me who needs convincing. Laura has been through a lot these past years. Some wounds take longer to heal than others. You will have to be patient." Emer bit her lip before asking him, "Do you know why they went to the sheriff?"

"Not really, Miss Emer, but thank you."

"Me? For what?"

"I am going to go courting Miss Murphy and be patient, just as you said."

CHAPTER 23

"Afternoon, Mrs. Higgins. Would it be possible to speak to Miss Murphy, please?" Paul fought to stop his voice from squeaking. Mrs. Higgins gave him an appraising look, but he thought she went off with a smile on her face.

Paul had rehearsed his speech over and over. He didn't want to get all tongue tied in front of Miss Murphy. Even thinking of her had him breaking out in a sweat. She was the most beautiful woman he had ever seen. Why would she look twice at a man like him? She might prefer Aaron or Samuel, but they were thinking of going to California and he guessed Miss Murphy would prefer to stay with her friends.

"Good afternoon, Mr. Kelley."

Paul tried his best to speak, but his tongue was stuck to the top of his mouth. He swallowed, but it didn't work. He saw amusement in her eyes as he stood there staring at her.

"Miss Murphy, you look very pretty today."

She smiled in response but didn't say anything. He moved from one foot to the other. *Just ask her.*

"I was wondering if you would like to come on a picnic. Davy will lend us his wagon. You can see a bit of the countryside. It's right pretty down by the creek."

"I can't, sorry." She turned to go back inside. Paul panicked.

"Wait, Miss Murphy. Why won't you come with me? We can ask someone to come with us if you would like a chaperone." He tried not to sound disappointed at the thought of someone joining them. He wanted to be alone with her.

"I hadn't thought of the chaperone," Laura said quietly, her face flaming.

"Why can't you come then?" He took a step closer but resisted the urge to stroke her face. He didn't want to scare her.

"Mr. Kelley, we were both embarrassed by Mary yesterday. I appreciate you calling on me, but I don't need anyone's pity."

"Pity? I don't pity you, Miss Murphy. I like you. A lot."

Laura stared at him, disbelief evident in her eyes.

"You don't know me."

"Well, that's true. I was hoping to rectify that a little by spending some time with you." He waited to see her reaction. She didn't look convinced. "Look, Miss Murphy, your friends came to Clover Springs and married men they didn't know. It seems to have worked out very well for the Sullivans and Petersens. Katie and Daniel are happy, too, although I know their story is slightly different. Miss Emer didn't know Mr. Shipley that long before they got married."

He stopped talking. It was the longest speech he had ever made and he wasn't sure she was listening.

"They all wanted to get married," Laura said.

"So do I," he replied. At the look of surprise on her face, he took her hand. "I had a whole speech prepared, but I forgot it as soon as I saw you. I asked Miss Emer to write to Boston and get me a bride. I never thought someone like you would land in Clover Springs. I would be honored if you would become my wife."

Laura pulled her hand back, panic on her face.

"Please, Miss Murphy, give me a chance. I don't know what happened to you before, but I would never hurt you. I just want to love you and protect you."

Why are you asking me? Laura wanted to believe him, she really did, but she couldn't trust her instincts. But everyone else liked him, too. Mary wouldn't encourage a friendship unless she approved. But she couldn't shake the idea that he was only acting out of pity. He could have any woman he wanted. He was tall and pleasant looking, clean shaven and he bathed regularly. Why would he settle for a woman with a reputation like hers? She had only gone into town a couple of times, but she had seen how the townsfolk stared at her. Conversations stopped when she walked into the store. Women moved closer to their menfolk. What did they think she was going to do, fling herself at any man she came in contact with?

"Miss Murphy?"

She watched as he took her hand in his, waiting for her body to shudder in revulsion, but it didn't. His touch had the opposite effect. It calmed her racing thoughts. She felt peaceful. She stared up into his face. His eyes were wide open, willing her to trust him. Could she?

"Maybe it's too early. I'm willing to wait until you are ready. I won't give up, though, Miss Murphy. Not until you agree to be my wife."

His wife. Mrs. Paul Kelley. That had a nice ring. She smiled at him as he bowed formally and walked away whistling. Now he was gone, she desperately wanted to run after him and say yes to the picnic. But she couldn't. It wasn't proper. One thing her experiences in Boston had taught her was that men liked to do the chasing. Maybe she could let Mr. Kelley court her like a real lady. Smiling widely, she turned and went back into the house.

CHAPTER 24

"Miss Laura, there's a wagon coming. Must be one of the ladies coming to visit. I've flour all over my hands. Could you go out to greet them, please?"

"Yes, Mrs. H." Laura went to the door smiling. Her arm was feeling much better and she was gradually getting more use of it. The exercises the doc had given her were painful, but she kept doing them.

"Laura, I need your help."

"Morning, Sorcha. How are you? I'm fine, thank you." Laura couldn't resist teasing. Sorcha wasn't pale, so it couldn't be an emergency that had her out at the Sullivans. She hadn't been driving fast.

"Sorry. I should remember my manners." Sorcha took Laura's arm and led her over to the chairs Mary had set out on the porch. "Sorry, I have to sit. My legs swell if I stand for too long. Having babies isn't pretty, you know."

Laura didn't answer. How could she? She hadn't been pregnant long enough to show like Sorcha did. Sorcha didn't know about the baby, so she hadn't actually been expecting an answer. She waited for Sorcha to speak again.

"Miss Freeman, the school teacher, has to leave Clover Springs. She was leaving anyway to get married, but that was supposed to be in a couple of months. Ellen would have known more about her plans by then. But Miss Freeman's parents were in an accident. She is getting the train to Denver tomorrow."

"The poor lady. I haven't met her yet, but I wouldn't wish that on anyone. What do you need me to do?"

"Teach the children. Ellen is still in Boulder. There is no one else."

"Me? Teach? Sorry, Sorcha, but you're dreaming. I can't teach, and even if I could, nobody will want their kids being taught by me."

"That's nonsense and you know it. You have more knowledge in your head than anyone."

Laura sat, biting her knuckle. Finally, she found her voice to ask, "Why can't Ellen come back and teach them?"

"Ellen studied really hard and Miss Freeman had to

arrange this introduction. It wouldn't be fair to call her back when you are here to fill in. Come on, Laura. You would be helping everyone."

"What if they hate me?" *What if their parents run me out of town?*

"Laura, when have children ever hated you? I know you aren't big on cuddles, but you are always fair. Kids liked and respected you at the orphanage. You can do this standing on your head. You know you can."

Laura didn't share Sorcha's confidence. "I don't know, Sorcha."

"It's very simple. Are you willing to help the people of Clover Springs or not? We helped you, didn't we?"

"Pulling the guilt card? That's hardly fair."

Sorcha took Laura's arm to help her out of the chair. She then led her back into Mary's house. "Maybe not, but it worked, didn't it? You will teach, won't you?"

Laura found herself agreeing. Not that she should be surprised. Sorcha had always been able to get her to do things. Teaching school. What would Mr. Kelley think? Would he approve of her being a teacher?

* * *

Paul rode up to the Sullivans' just as Laura was getting in the wagon.

"You're off early, Miss Murphy."

"Laura has agreed to teach school. Isn't that wonderful?" Sorcha said.

"I didn't know you were a teacher." Paul looked at Laura.

"I'm not, but they were desperate. The teacher had a family emergency and Katie's sister, Ellen, is still away in Boulder. So they got stuck with me." Her tone sounded flippant, but he thought he heard a hint of nervousness in her voice.

He wanted to pull her into his arms and tell her how lucky the children would be to have her as a teacher. What was he thinking? If he tried to touch her, he'd scare her or she'd slap him for ungentlemanly behavior. She was a city lady and he was a country cowboy.

"I am sure that's not true. There are a few women I could name who would volunteer to teach school. They must think you are the right woman for the job."

Laura nodded, but Paul could see the doubt and uncertainty in her eyes. Whoever had destroyed her confidence really did a great job. Some of the children in the school would eat her alive if they sensed she was nervous.

"Just be yourself and watch out for the Shaw boy and the Hawthorns. Boys and girls. Those kids are a handful."

"Thank you, Mr. Kelley. I have to go now. Sorcha is giving me a lift to town."

"I will be in town later. I'll stop by to escort you home, if that is okay with you?"

He noted the pink flush in her cheeks as her eyes glanced at his mouth before staring back at him. *She does like me.*

"It's a long walk back, and as I am driving past here anyway, it seems a pity not to take advantage of me."

"Take advantage of you?" Laura chuckled, the sound making the hair on the back of his neck stand up. He could listen to her laughing all day long.

"Yes, Ma'am." He watched the indecision play in her eyes, as the slight breeze caused red tendrils of hair to frame her face. *Go on, take a chance. Say yes.*

"Well, in that case, how could I refuse?"

"See you this afternoon then. Have a good day." He helped her into the buckboard and then stood watching until it disappeared from view.

"You going to stand there all day?"

Embarrassed, Paul turned to find Davy and some of the other men looking at him, amused grins on their faces. Davy handed him a coffee.

"Nope. I got work to be doing. Don't you?"

The grin Davy sent him showed his friend knew Paul's attraction to Miss Murphy was real. *Does he know I intend on making her my wife?* Maybe he should ask Davy for some tips on courting Miss Murphy. His boss had married a mail order bride, and despite some initial hurdles, they seemed happily married now. Paul looked at Davy before deciding not to say anything. Davy was a great boss, but they were hardly confidants. He had work to do.

Paul swallowed his coffee. He wanted to get to work quickly to keep his promise to collect Laura from town. He had only taken the job because it gave him a reason to visit the ranch on a daily basis, and now she was working in town as a teacher. His face clouded.

Everything said Laura Murphy wasn't the right woman for him. He was a carpenter and ranch hand; she was educated well enough to be a teacher. Ma would never approve, for one thing, but that didn't stop him thinking of her all day long.

CHAPTER 25

"Good morning, children, this is my friend Miss Murphy. She is going to be your teacher until Miss O'Callaghan returns from Boulder. Can we all say good morning, please?"

"Good morning, Miss Murphy."

The sing-song response of the children did nothing for Laura's nerves. She wiped her hands down the side of her skirt again. Why had she let the other girls talk her into this?

She sent a frantic look at Sorcha, but her friend just smiled and closed the school door behind her. Laura turned to face the class once more.

"Good morning. I am new to Clover Springs, so you will all have to be a little patient with me. I don't know your names. Perhaps you could write them on your slates. Put them on your desk for me and I will do my best to learn them." Having a great memory worked out well sometimes. Laura moved down the aisle separating the two rows of desks. Most of the children had complied with her request, but a couple of the boys hadn't started to write.

"Is there a problem?"

"No, Miss." The boy who answered her looked her up and down in such a cheeky manner, Laura was shocked into silence. It took her a couple of seconds to remember her chance of managing the classroom depended on dealing with troublemakers before they got a chance to make trouble.

"Oh, I see. You need help writing your name?" Laura kept her tone as sweet as possible, eyeing the boy as the rest of the children laughed.

"I ain't dumb. I can write my own name."

"I am not dumb." At his confused look, she explained. "You said *I ain't,* but the correct way to say it is *I am not.*"

"I don't have to listen to you. You aren't a real teacher. Anyone can see that."

"What's your name?"

"Shaw. Bertram Shaw."

One of the kids Mr. Kelley had warned her about.

"Well, Mr. Shaw, you are both correct and incorrect. I may not be the usual teacher, but I am currently in charge of this class. I won't allow insubordination in my classroom. Please do as I ask or take yourself to the corner and stand there for five minutes."

"I don't have to."

"Ten minutes."

"I'm not doing what you say and none of the rest of them is either."

"Fifteen minutes. If you haven't worked it out yet, Mr. Shaw, you will spend the entire day on your feet with your back to the class. Or you can choose to write your name now. Your choice."

The class fell silent, watching the battle of wills.

"Twenty minutes, Mr. Shaw, and if you make me wait any longer, recess will be cancelled, as I will have fallen behind in my schedule."

"Do as Laura, I mean Miss Murphy, says. I don't want to miss recess."

"Thank you, Ben."

"Nobody going to listen to no cripple. Are you?" Bertram Shaw's confident stance faltered as he was greeted with silence from the rest of the class.

"Given your appalling manners, poor grammar and inconsiderate approach to your fellow students, I believe some extra time in school will do you the world of good. You will remain for thirty minutes after school."

"You can't do that. Ma will kill you."

"I doubt that, Mr. Shaw. Now please let us move

on. Write your name on your slate. Although, after this morning, I don't think I will have trouble remembering it."

The class exploded into laughter as Bertram Shaw, red as a flame, wrote his name on the slate. Then he remained sitting.

Laura coughed and discretely nodded to the corner. With bad grace, he stood up, muttering, and moved to stand in the corner.

Smiling, Laura walked back toward the teacher's desk. That might teach him for being mean to Little Beaver, Ben, and goodness knows who else.

The day passed without further incident. She was enjoying herself more than she ever thought possible. The children had open minds and were eager to learn. She had taken a quick look at their textbooks the night before. Remembering how dull she had found lessons, she tried to make her class interesting and fun. Judging by the reactions of the students, her plan had worked.

"Excuse me, Miss, but are you coming back tomorrow?"

"When is our teacher coming back?" a girl lisped through her missing front teeth.

"Yes, Steven. I will be here until Miss O'Callaghan or Miss Freeman returns." Laura focused on the girl.

"Sorry, Meg, but I don't know when your teacher will be back."

Steven beamed in response before realizing both of his and Meg's slates were turned to the blank side. "Wow, Miss, you have a good memory. You couldn't see our names."

"Laura's special. She can memorize all sorts of books and… Sorry, Miss Murphy. I forgot." Ben's face flushed as the children looked from him to her and back again.

"Don't worry, Ben, and no harm done." Laura crossed her fingers, hoping she was right. Only time would tell. She looked over the students and found Bertram Shaw staring back at her, a look of devilish delight on his face. He meant trouble.

What can a child do to you? Laura gave herself a talking to, despite feeling like someone had just walked over her grave. It was time for the children to go home. After they had all run outside, Laura tidied up for a few minutes before walking out the door to find the boys waiting for her. They weren't the only ones waiting.

"Afternoon, Miss Murphy. I promised you a ride back to the Sullivans'."

"Can we come, too, Mr. Kelley? It's a long walk in the heat."

Laura hid a smile as Ben and the other children

looked imploringly at Paul. He sent her a look before sighing with defeat.

"Jump in the back. Hold on tight, though." Paul got down and walked over to where Laura was standing. "You survived the first day."

"Barely. The Shaw boy was everything you said and more. Thank you for the warning. I was ready for him."

"I think you could handle most anybody, Miss Murphy."

His words were lovely, but it was the look in his eyes that made her miss her step. He caught her before she fell, holding her for a few seconds. She thought he was going to kiss her. The women of the town would have a fit. She coughed, causing him to color slightly before helping her into the wagon.

She tried hard not to touch him as they drove home, but the bumps of the road had other ideas. They hit one particularly large dip, causing her to fall against him. He laughed.

"One might think you did that on purpose, Mr. Kelley," she said, using her schoolteacher's voice.

"Not at all, Miss Murphy."

She moved back slightly to put a decent distance between them, but the gap was narrower than before. He glanced at her, his eyes smiling, causing her to flush once more. She liked him and knew he liked her, but still she couldn't bring herself to say yes. From what Mary had told her, his mother would never agree to a match between them. His ma wasn't the only obstacle. She couldn't shake the fear he would change once they were married. Johnny had. *Johnny didn't change,* she scolded herself. *You just didn't see him for what he was until it was too late.*

CHAPTER 26

Laura almost sang as she walked to school the next morning. She had an idea for a quiz and wanted to have it all set up before the children arrived.

She couldn't believe how inspired she was. Learning had always come easy to her; it was one of the advantages of having a mind like hers. But she had found school boring. She wanted to make it a different experience for the children of Clover Springs. It hadn't taken long to see there were a couple of bright children in the school. Keeping them interested would be as much of a challenge as helping the less able children to improve.

She wrote her questions on the board, a smile playing around her lips as she imagined the looks of delight when the children arrived. Soon she heard

Davy's voice outside as he dropped off Meggie, Jenny, Ben and Little Beaver. Nandita's children weren't far behind them. Steven came in somewhat later, but he didn't return Laura's smile.

"Miss Murphy, sorry, I shouldn't be here, but I had to tell you. I can't stay in school."

He couldn't look at her while talking to her, but shifted from foot to foot.

"Why?"

"Mrs. Shaw told Pa he'd get no more work from her if he kept us in school. He doesn't have enough customers to tell her to get lost, but I think he would if he could. Pa doesn't like a woman telling him what to do."

"Thank you for coming, Steven."

"I like you as a teacher. I don't care what Mrs. Shaw says. Yesterday was fun."

He was gone before Laura could react.

"This is all my fault, isn't it, Laura? I couldn't keep my big mouth shut."

"Hush up, Ben. This isn't anyone's fault. We don't know why Mrs. Shaw has seen fit to stop children coming to school. It could be for any number of reasons."

My past, my hair, my gift or just simply me.

"Why don't we continue our lessons? I prepared a quiz for you with prizes for the best answers. Who wants to go first?"

The three children and Little Beaver stared at her.

"Why don't you go and tell Mrs. Shaw she's wrong?" Little Beaver asked.

"People believe what they want to. You can't change their minds."

"You can try. You said yesterday education opens our minds. Were you telling lies?"

"No, of course not." Laura spoke too sharply. "I apologize, Little Beaver. My tone was uncalled for."

He crossed his arms, looking older than he was. For a second, Laura could see him as an Indian brave of years gone past, so fierce was his expression.

"You are afraid of this woman. She is too powerful for you."

"No. She isn't powerful."

"So why are you letting her win without even trying to fight her?"

Laura stood, looking at the four faces staring back at her. Why was she not doing anything? All her life, she had fought back to some extent—until Johnny. He had taken everything from her. It was time to take back her self-respect.

"Little Beaver, watch the children. Teach them math or something. I won't be long."

"Yes, Ma'am."

Laura strode out of the school and off to find Mrs.

Shaw. She had no idea where to find the lady in question, so she decided to go to the store. Pushing the door open, she found a group of ladies. Given the sudden silence and Katie's red face, she guessed they had been discussing her.

"Mrs. Shaw, I believe you have an issue with how I run my classroom." Laura went straight in on the attack. It wouldn't do any good to show this bully she was scared of her. Bullies fed on feeling powerful and in control.

"Well? Are you going to tell me what the issue is? If I know, maybe I can resolve it and return to teaching the children."

"I don't have to explain myself to you. You should never have been put in charge of a room full of children. Nobody knows anything about you. You could be anyone."

"I know Miss Murphy, and I vouched for her character," Katie said loudly.

"Yes, well, we all know that you have lower standards than we would like, Mrs. Sullivan." Mrs. Shaw's younger companion sniggered at her own remark.

Katie glared so hard, Laura thought her eyes would burst out of their sockets.

"Miss Hawthorn, please try your best to remain civil. I know it is difficult for you."

Laura had to fight not to smile as Katie's sarcasm

hit home. So this was the woman Mrs. Kelley had picked out for Paul. No wonder he had run away. Not only was she older, but her pinched little face and cold eyes made her look mean. *Laura Murphy, you shouldn't judge anyone by how they look.*

Laura looked at the group of women, examining each one. Any open attack would have them circling the wagons and retreating for protection. She had to find another approach.

"I apologize, Mrs. Shaw." *Good, that got their attention.* "I was under the impression nobody else was available to teach school. The children would, of course, greatly benefit from your teaching. Would you like me to leave the copy of the lesson plans I prepared, or would you prefer to use your own?"

"Pardon? I am not going to teach. I have… things to do."

Laura pretended to be confused. "Oh, I'm sorry. I thought you wanted to teach. Who would you have run the school instead?" She caught a glimpse of amusement on Katie's face.

"I would like to hear the answer to that question, too."

Laura looked at the older woman who had walked into the store.

"Mrs. Grey, you know how I feel about this… woman. I spoke to Mrs. Kelley only yesterday. We discussed her lack of credentials. We don't even know if she can read or write. She didn't read a book at any point during the day yesterday but seemed to rely on her memory for everything."

"Is this true, Miss Murphy?"

"I can read and write, but yes, I didn't use any books. I had everything stored in my head before class started."

"Did the children enjoy their lessons? Did they make any progress? Although it would be hard to judge *anyone* on the basis of one day."

"The children told me they had fun," Laura murmured.

"Fun! School isn't supposed to be entertainment. They are there to learn and work hard."

"I agree, Mrs. Shaw."

"You do?" Mrs. Shaw looked totally confused as Laura smiled and nodded.

"Yes, of course. I believe children can have fun while learning. In fact, I would go so far as to say they would remember more if we made lessons less boring."

"I agree, Miss Murphy. It can be hard to concentrate in this heat. A lot of the children are already tired by the time they have walked to school. I remember falling asleep over my books more than once," Mrs. Grey smiled.

"Me too," Katie chimed in.

"No, this simply won't do. You don't understand, Lorena. Bertram told me she didn't open one book. How can you teach children anything without books? She also struggled to control the class. They kept laughing."

In response to Mrs. Grey's questioning look, Laura responded quietly. "I did have a discipline issue, but I believe that problem is now taken care of."

"See, she admits she lost control. What sort of teacher is she?" Mrs. Shaw looked at the other ladies, but they didn't seem to be as openly supportive as before.

They looked to Mrs. Grey, who in turn was looking at Laura.

"Why didn't you cane the child in question, Miss Murphy?"

Despite herself, Laura flinched at the thought of beating a child. It was something she could never do.

"Laura attended the same orphanage as Mary, Sorcha and Ben. She saw many beatings and other examples of child cruelty. Having seen the effects of that firsthand, I doubt Miss Murphy could inflict it on a child," Katie answered.

Laura sent her a relieved glance, which was intercepted by Mrs. Grey.

"I sent the child in question to the corner. Initially,

he refused to go, but in the end, he did. I do not believe he would defy me as openly as before. I am not suggesting he has turned into a well-mannered young man. His grammar skills match those of his behavior." Laura didn't miss the gleam of approval in Mrs. Grey's eyes. Emboldened, she continued, "With time and perhaps a lot of patience, I think progress could be made."

"I like your common sense approach. I think you should go back to teaching school, Miss Murphy."

Laura sighed a little too loudly, causing a small titter of laughter. But it wasn't aimed in a nasty way.

"Wait, what about her not using books? She can't teach without them," Mrs. Shaw whined.

"Perhaps you should leave the teaching to Miss Murphy and spend some time putting your own house in order. Excuse us, ladies. I have some other business to attend to." Mrs. Grey walked out of the store. As she got to the door, she turned back. "Miss Murphy, are you coming or not? I'd like to hear more about this amazing mind of yours."

Laura almost laughed aloud as the other ladies stared, open-mouthed. She let the door close behind her.

"Thank you for what you did in the store, Mrs. Grey."

"Small minds can be mean and nasty. So can their

children. I never had any time for Bertram Shaw. He is a bully, just like his mother." Mrs. Grey eyed her speculatively. Laura wanted to bite her knuckle but resisted by folding her hands under her arms. "I met a doctor who could memorize whole text books just by reading them once."

Laura couldn't hide her surprise. "Like me?"

"Yes, my dear. Just like you, although believe me, he wasn't blessed with your good looks. He was a fine man. A gifted doctor."

They walked toward the direction of the school.

"It's an easier gift for a man to deal with. But it is a gift you have. I think it is wonderful you are using it to help children learn. Only with more education and understanding of all types of people will our great country thrive. Have a good day, Miss Murphy."

Mrs. Grey kept walking this time, leaving Laura in the middle of the street with her mouth hanging open.

CHAPTER 27

"Morning, Katie. Laura told me what happened in the store yesterday." Mary faltered, her eyes darting from Katie to Emer.

Katie coughed. She hated to be the bearer of bad news, but it was time to tell Laura.

"Father Molloy sent a telegram. We need to warn Laura."

Mary gestured her inside. "I'll go call her. Go into the sitting room. Mrs. H was up with the larks this morning."

"Something smells very good," Katie said, more for something to say in an attempt to lift the charged atmosphere.

Laura entered the sitting room closely followed by Mary.

"Katie, Emer, what's wrong?"

Katie saw the alarm and tension in her friend's face.

"Yes, it's trouble, Laura. Your friend came to see Father Molloy again, so he wanted to know if you had married. Seems some man called Coleman has been asking questions about you."

Laura paled as she stared at Katie. Katie moved to take Laura's hand and led her gently to the couch, forcing her to sit down. "Laura, darling, don't be afraid. Nobody is going to hurt you in Clover Springs."

"Who's threatening Miss Murphy? If it's that Bertram Shaw, I'll put him over my knee and cane him myself."

Katie and Emer exchanged a quick look as Paul Kelley and Davy came into the room.

"Sorry for intruding, ladies. Davy asked me to put up some shelves in his office. I didn't mean to listen in on your conversation, but I was hoping to speak to Miss Murphy. Now I won't leave until I find out what's wrong."

Katie opened her mouth but closed it again once she saw Emer eyeing Paul. She had a gleam in her eyes and a smile on her face.

"Miss Murphy has to get married. As soon as possible. Her life could be in danger."

"She'll marry me. I won't let anyone hurt her."

"Well said, Kelley, but perhaps you should ask her

rather than tell us?" Davy winked at Paul, who colored considerably.

The poor man. He obviously forgot we were all here.

* * *

She couldn't breathe. Coleman was looking for her. Why? Her stomach was all knotted up. What could she do? She didn't want to leave Clover Springs. She had grown to love the town and its people in the short time she'd been here. She held her belly as the pain shot through her. For the first time, she had found somewhere she belonged. She was happy. Why was life so unfair?

"Miss Murphy, listen to me. You have no choice. Marry me. I love you. I will wait however long it takes for you to believe in me. In us."

She forced herself to look at him. She could see he believed what he was saying, but could she take the chance? What if her instinct was wrong? Again. She didn't think she'd survive another marriage like her first. He took her hand and pulled her into the corner of the room. The others started talking loudly amongst themselves in a rather obvious attempt to convince her they weren't watching every second of their exchange.

"I'm not him," he whispered so nobody else could hear him. "Our marriage will be in name only."

Her head jerked up at that.

"Not forever, I hope." He caressed her hand gently. "I'll wait until you are ready. I want you to love me even though I love you enough for the both of us. Stay in Clover Springs. Marry me."

She squeezed her eyes shut, hoping for a voice of reason, but there was only silence.

"Laura, I promise I will never do or say anything to hurt you. I will keep you safe. Open your eyes and look at me."

She stared up at him. He was kind and patient. He was strong and resourceful, honest and… "Yes."

"Yes you will stay, or yes you will marry me?"

"Both." She smiled up at him shyly.

He embraced her, lifting her off her feet and twirling her in the air. She burst out laughing. The pain in her stomach had disappeared.

"She said yes!" he shouted over to their friends, who had given them a little space.

"We guessed," Davy said drily, making everyone laugh.

Emer walked toward them, engulfing Paul in a hug. "It's about time," she whispered. "Now, go see Reverend Timmons before she gets spooked again."

CHAPTER 28

"You are not marrying her. Take her back to the Sullivans'."

"Ma, watch your tone. I am going to marry Miss Murphy and we are going to live here. This is my homestead, not yours."

"So you are going to throw your crippled old ma out on the street. All because some floozy caught your eye."

"Ma, keep a respectful tongue in your head. Miss Murphy is going to be my wife."

"Paul, take me back to the Sullivans'. Please. Your ma is entitled to her opinion. This was a mistake." Laura moved to leave, but Paul put his hand out to stop her.

"Ma, this is my place. I picked Laura as my wife. You are welcome to live here if you accept her and treat her properly." Paul sent what he hoped was a smile of reassurance in Laura's direction before turning his full gaze on his ma. "Ma, apologize to Miss Murphy and we will forget about this little outburst."

"Well, I—"

"Ma. I mean it. Miss Murphy has had enough to deal with. As soon as we are married, this home will be her sanctuary. Somewhere she will be free. Nobody, not even you, is going to stop me from providing that for her."

"The rumors must be true. You have cast some sort of spell on my boy, madam. I will not let you have him."

Laura took a step back from the vindictiveness in the older woman's eyes. For a supposedly frail house-bound lady, she had a strong voice and an even stronger will. She kicked herself for thinking this would be different. Why would any mother want their child involved with her? She mightn't like Mrs. Kelley's attitude, but she couldn't blame her for wanting to protect Paul.

"I want to go now," Laura said quietly to Paul before removing his hold from her arm. "Your ma has made her feelings clear. Good afternoon, Mrs. Kelley."

"Good riddance."

Laura didn't acknowledge the response, deciding it best to pretend she hadn't heard her. She didn't look at

Paul, but she knew he was angry. She had seen him holding himself in check when his ma launched into her rant. She admired him for standing up for her, but he deserved a better life than the one she could offer. He would be a good father and husband. She didn't want to picture him with anyone other than her and certainly not Miss Hawthorn. She was so like Ma Kelley, they could be mistaken for mother and daughter.

* * *

"LAURA, stay where you are. Ma, I love you and respect you as my mother, but do not make me chose between you and the woman I love. I will marry Laura."

"Not under my roof you won't."

Paul couldn't look at Laura. He was transfixed by the look of satisfaction on his mother's face.

"Yes, you heard me. This is my homestead and my land. I made your father put my name on the deed. You never thought to check, you imbecile. You just assumed it was yours. And I let you." Ma Kelley cackled so loudly, Paul wondered if she had lost her sanity.

"I won't see you marry that trollop."

Taking a deep breath, Paul moved to Laura's side. "Let me escort you to the wagon."

He took a grip of her arm and pushed her toward the door.

"That's it. Throw her off my property."

"She's leaving, Ma, and so am I."

"What?" Both women spoke at once.

"Paul, don't do this. I'm not worth it," Laura said quietly. His heart twisted at the tears in her eyes, but he was proud of the fact she hadn't cried in front of his mother.

"You heard her. She isn't fit to be a Kelley."

Paul moved about the cabin, quickly gathering a couple of items.

"Goodbye, Ma."

Without as much as a backward look, he steered Laura out the door and toward the wagon. His mother screeched and screamed behind them, but he ignored her. She had ruled his life for years.

"I'm sorry, Laura. I shouldn't have brought you here. My mother is… her sanity is questionable."

"You should go back in and fix things with your ma. You can't walk away from all this." Laura threw her arms out, gesturing to the land.

He held his gaze to hers. "I am not throwing away anything of value. I told you, I love you. I am going to marry you. I have a job with the Sullivans and somewhere to stay, too. I am a good carpenter."

Laura stood, transfixed. He could see the questions

in her eyes. Was he seriously going to walk away from his family and land for her? Could he really love her that much? *Yes and yes, my darling.*

"Laura, look at me. I can see your doubts as if you spoke them out loud. We are going to have a long and happy life together. I don't care what happened in your past, or what secrets you have yet to tell me. All I know is I love you and I think you care for me. In time, I hope you will come to trust your feelings. And to trust me with your heart." He moved to hold her gently by the shoulders, drawing her closer to him. "Now let's go ask Reverend Timmons to bring the wedding forward. Let's get married tomorrow. We don't need to worry about appearances. By the time Ma is done, the whole town will know you cast a spell on me."

Her head jerked up, but he was smiling. Teasing her. Before she could say anything, he bent and kissed her lightly on the lips, whispering, "A spell I welcome."

CHAPTER 29

Laura nibbled her knuckle the whole way back to the Sullivan ranch. What were they going to do? Where would they live? Was Paul really going to throw away his future just for her?

"Laura, stop frowning. We are going to be fine. We will find a place to stay. I should have done this years ago. I hate farming."

"But your ma is all alone. She won't be able to manage the farm by herself."

He leaned down, his lips lightly grazing the top of her head.

"Ma will be fine. You'll see. She has enough money saved to hire on some workers. She may just find she's not as frail as she thought she was."

Laura didn't respond. They were back at Mary's. Her friends were going to be upset on her behalf.

"There you are. Emer and Lawrence came by earlier. We waited for you to come back so we could all have dinner together. To celebrate." Mary's voice trailed off. "What's wrong now? Laura, don't tell me you called off the wedding. I know you are not keen on getting married again, but you have to."

"Ma threw her out." Paul jumped down before walking around to help Laura. He put his arms around her waist. She inhaled deeply. He kept his arm around her as they walked to the house. She was grateful for his quiet support. The encounter with his mother had left her more shaken than she realized.

"What? Why? She doesn't know anything about you." Mary faltered. "I mean, oh, you know what I mean. Come inside and forget about her. She probably just needs time to think things through."

"She threw us both off her land. We don't have anywhere to live now."

Mary didn't speak, but Davy, who had come out to greet them, answered for her.

"You can both live here for now. There's a small house further out on the ranch. Grandpa built it when he first came to Clover Springs. Harry and Lizzie lived in it for a while, too, until they got their new home built. It's in good shape. We can go out now and have a look at it if you want, Kelley?"

Paul squeezed Laura's hand gently. "Thank you, Davy. It is mighty generous of you. We could use it until we figure out whether we are going to stay in town or start our own homestead. If Laura's agreeable, that is."

Laura smiled as she hugged Mary. "Thank you, both of you."

"Come in and help me. Don't be long, boys, or Mrs. H may decide not to feed you."

"In that case, race you, Kelley." Davy took off running with Paul chasing after him. The women laughed.

"What is it about men? They never seem to grow up," Mary said, poking Laura in the ribs. "Hey, you, stop staring at your groom-to-be."

KNOCKING at the door dragged Laura from her thoughts. Today was her wedding day. She had been dreaming of her first wedding. It had been a rushed affair too. Johnny had said he didn't believe in God and had persuaded her she didn't need or want a church wedding. Instead, they had been married with two witnesses, neither of whom she had met before. *Stop it. Paul isn't Johnny.*

She opened her eyes to see Mary coming through

the door. Mrs. H followed right behind her, carrying a green dress. She sat up straighter in bed.

"Are you going to lie there all day?" Mary teased, a big smile on her face. Mrs. H draped the dress over the back of the chair.

"Where did that come from?"

"Mrs. H and I made it for you as soon as you agreed to marry Paul. We knew you didn't have anything suitable. It's our wedding present."

"Oh Mary, it's amazing." Laura jumped out of the bed to feel the material. "It's the nicest dress I've ever seen."

"Try it on. We don't have much time to make sure it fits. We don't want to keep Paul waiting. The poor boy is suffering enough as it is." Mrs. H picked at a thread on the dress.

Did he regret proposing? Had his Ma convinced him he was doing the wrong thing? That it was a mistake to marry her?

The dress fit perfectly, although Mrs. H kept fussing until Laura was fit to scream. She tied her hair back, leaving a couple of curls to accent her face.

Mary left them alone. She had to dress Cathy and change into her own wedding outfit. Laura didn't know who was more excited—her or Mary, who was her matron of honor.

"Paul Kelley will make you a fine husband, Miss

Laura." Mrs. H smiled at her through the looking glass. "I know you are nervous. Given what you have been through, it's understandable. But believe me. You let the man love you and you will bloom like a rose in my garden."

"I'll try," Laura whispered.

Mrs. H caressed her shoulder gently. "You got to let go of the past, Miss Laura. Only way you will be happy. Stop letting your demons steal your future."

Laura only nodded. It wasn't appropriate to tell the older woman how she was feeling. The thought of Paul holding her scared her senseless. What if he was just the same as her first husband? *But he isn't. He's shown you over and over.*

"Laura, you ready? Davy says it's time to go," Mary called from outside the door.

Laura picked up the bouquet Mrs. H had prepared for her. "Thank you so much for everything, Mrs. H." She leaned in and kissed the older woman. "See you at the church."

"Oh no, Miss Laura. I have to stay here and make sure your wedding breakfast is ready."

"Mrs. H, I am not getting married unless you are in the church with me." Laura sat on the bed as Mary walked through the door.

"Miss Mary, tell her I can't go."

"I'll do nothing of the sort. You are like family, Mrs.

H, and you should be there. We will all help with the food when we get back. Now go get changed. You can't let Reverend Timmons see that old dress."

The two younger women smiled as Mrs. H realized she was beaten and went to change. She didn't take long. Laura pulled a flower out of her bouquet and pinned it to the older woman's dress. "Thank you. I feel braver knowing you will be there."

She saw tears in the older woman's eyes but pretended she hadn't. They jumped when Davy shouted they were going to be late. Laughing and hugging one another, they moved down the stairs and out the door. Stunned, Laura admired the flowers decorating the wagon.

"The children wanted to surprise you. Do you like it?"

"I love it. Thank you everyone." Laura beamed.

Her good humor vanished when they arrived at the church. There was no sign of anyone else. Had he run away?

"Relax Laura. He's waiting inside. He told Davy he was going to leave his wagon at the store. He didn't want any unwelcome guests."

Laura took Davy's arm as he helped her out of the wagon and into the church. "Mary gave me permission to walk you down the aisle if you would like me to."

Laura blinked to clear the tears from her eyes. She

held his arm tightly as they walked slowly up to where Paul stood waiting. He was smiling but she couldn't respond. She had to concentrate on breathing, fighting the panic.

"You look beautiful, Laura," Paul whispered as Davy let her arm go. She swayed for a couple of seconds. *Breathe. You can do this.*

"Miss Murphy, are you ready?"

Laura glanced at Reverend Timmons but she didn't answer. She looked at Paul, her lips moving but no words coming out.

"Laura, can I speak to you for a moment? Excuse us, Reverend."

Laura let Paul guide her to the front of the church away from the rest of the guests. "Laura, I know this isn't what you planned. You have to get married. I will do my best to be the husband you deserve. I love you. I know you find it hard to believe but I promise, as God is my witness, I will never treat you badly."

She looked up into his face, the truth of his words shining from his eyes. He meant everything he said.

"Are you ready?" He whispered offering her his hand.

You have to let the demons go, Laura. Mrs. H's words filled her mind.

"Yes, Paul. I am."

The rest of the ceremony passed in a blur. She said

her lines and at the end, Paul kissed her. His lips grazed hers but didn't linger, leaving her wanting more. She didn't get time to dwell on her reaction as her friends hugged her, wishing them both well. Everyone was smiling. She was a married woman again but this time, she was surrounded by those who wanted her to be happy. It would be different this time. Wouldn't it?

PAUL LOOKED at his bride as they rode back to the Sullivan ranch. She looked radiant in her new dress but her eyes glistened with tears. He prayed for strength and guidance to help her learn to trust him. He loved her and yearned to make her his. But a glance at her face proved now was not the time. He needed to take things slow. He promised her he wouldn't rush her or make her do anything she might regret. He intended to keep that promise regardless of how difficult it was not to touch her. She was his wife. But for now, she was his in name only. He drew the horse to a halt some distance from the house.

"Why did you stop?" She asked, her voice shaking.

"I just wanted a minute alone with my wife." He loved calling her that. He moved to brush a curl back from her face, immediately regretting his action as she pulled back. "Relax Laura, I won't do anything. I made you a promise. I keep my word."

Picking up the reins, he urged the horses on toward the house. He had known from the start this wasn't going to be easy. But until this moment, he hadn't realized just how big a task making his wife trust him was going to be.

CHAPTER 30

"Where are we going, Miss?"

"Little Beaver is going to show us how to survive in the wild. He's going to teach us how to make a fire and how to track animals."

"Are we going hunting?" Ben's face lit up with excitement.

"Not today, Ben." Laura hated disappointing the children, but she didn't think the parents would like her teaching them how to use knives and guns. That was not a group activity, but rather something for fathers to teach on a one-on-one basis.

"Don't see how this is educational. We don't need to know how to live like savages."

Laura bristled at the insult to Little Beaver and his people. "Bertram, the Indians are not savages. They can teach us a lot. They know how to survive on the land. I can't imagine you lasting very long if you were lost out there alone." Laura pointed toward the mountain range.

"My ma isn't going to like this. She doesn't agree with them being in our school."

Laura took them to mean Little Beaver and Nandita's children. She could well understand the look of fury on Little Beaver's face. He looked so fierce. She could imagine his ancestors scalping someone. Although, to be fair, she thought Bertram and his mother deserved to be tortured at length. *Stop that, Laura. It's not Christian.*

"Thankfully, your mother is not in charge of the school. I am. Today, we are going to learn some skills, and tomorrow there will be a test. Anyone, and that includes you, Mr. Shaw, who fails the test will have extra homework for the weekend."

"Shut up, Bertram. We have enough chores over the weekend. We don't need extra homework," Peter scolded Bertram. Judging by the looks of his classmates, he spoke for the whole school.

"Come on, everyone. Let's go have some fun. It's a beautiful day and we can enjoy a picnic." Laura cheered everyone on as they walked through town and headed toward the prairie.

"What do you want me to show them, Miss Laura?"

"That's up to you, Little Beaver. Today, you are the

teacher. But I don't expect you to subject anyone to torture, no matter how painful they become."

"Yes, Miss Laura."

Laura had to turn away to hide her smile at his downcast expression. He took so much abuse from Bertram and his cronies he was probably looking forward to making the boy pay today. Much as she understood, she couldn't condone bullying on any level.

The day was better than Laura had hoped for. The class was delighted to learn how to make a small fire. Little Beaver showed them how to make smoke signals and they had some fun sending messages home. Nobody told the younger kids their parents wouldn't be able to read them. Little Beaver showed them how to track an animal, although they didn't catch anything. They ended the afternoon with a picnic and a quick fishing expedition to the creek. Tired but happy, they headed back to town.

"Trouble, Miss Laura." Little Beaver's anxious tone caught Laura off guard. She had been too busy thinking about the fun they had to pay attention to the schoolhouse. She looked up to find a swarm of adults waiting for them. Her heart fell as she recognized Mrs. Shaw, Ida Hawthorn, and was that Mrs. Kelley? Although she should have been confined to her house, she didn't look very ill standing there with her arms on her hips.

"What is the meaning of this? Why aren't the children at school? Bertram, where are your shoes?"

Surprising herself, Laura sympathized with the boy. She'd seen him enjoying himself at the river once he got over his disdain for the so-called savages in the group. Now his mother was chastising him for having fun. For being a child.

Laura pushed Bertram behind her in an effort to protect him. After everything she had seen at the orphanage, she wasn't going to let anyone bully a child, not even that child's own mother.

"I took the class out on a learning expedition. It involved learning how to fish, so some of the children got wet, but they are all dry now. They tied their shoes around their necks so they wouldn't be ruined by the water. "

"Learning? More like a holiday. We do not send our children to school to go fishing." Mrs. Shaw puffed up her chest, her face contorted with anger.

"Ma, I told her you wouldn't like it. But she insisted Little Beaver teach us how to make a fire and track wild animals."

"Oh, my poor boy. You could have been killed. You, Miss Murphy, or whatever your name is, are a liability. You are not a fit teacher."

"I told you she's a witch. She doesn't behave like any teacher I ever met. She has the men of the town falling over her, including, I am sorry to say, my own son. He deserted me, left me working the homestead all by myself, just so he could be with her."

Laura instinctively took a step back from the venom spitting from Mrs. Kelley. At the same time, Little Beaver moved forward.

"Miss Laura is the best teacher ever. You should not speak about her like this."

Laura watched, horrified, as Mrs. Kelley lifted her hand to slap Little Beaver. The youth reacted by taking her hand and forcing it behind her back, causing her to howl with pain.

"Get the sheriff! I've been attacked!"

Bertram ran faster than Laura had ever seen him move before.

"Little Beaver, release Mrs. Kelley." When the boy hesitated, Laura insisted. He moved away from the group, but his gaze was locked to that of Ma Kelley.

"You saw what he did. Is that what you are teaching the rest of the children, how to behave like that savage?"

Laura put a protective arm around the boy. "Little Beaver did nothing wrong. You were going to strike him. He simply protected himself. It is you who the sheriff should arrest."

"How dare you? You saw what happened." Ma Kelley took a step closer to Laura, but she didn't withdraw this time. She stood her ground after taking the precaution of pushing Little Beaver behind her. The boy's temper was riled and she didn't want him doing anything they'd both regret.

"Ma, what on earth is going on here?"

Sweat poured down Laura's back at the sound of Paul's voice. She didn't take her eyes off Ma Kelley as her husband moved closer to them. His arm wrapped itself around her shoulders and she let herself relax into his side.

"Your witch of a wife took the children on a trip without their parents' consent. She said they were learning survival skills from that… boy." Ma Kelley's face was purple at this stage. "When I challenged her, the boy attacked me."

"Ma, you don't have any kids in the school. It's got nothing to do with you."

Laura almost giggled at the look on Ma Kelley's face.

"My wife knows what she is doing. The children in Clover Springs should be taught how to survive in any situation. This is the Wild West, not some city park. I have every faith in Little Beaver."

Laura had to resist hugging Paul. She could see the

impact of his praise on Little Beaver, who stood to the side, his body poised for battle.

"Paul, he attacked me. You are not going to stand by and let that go unpunished." Ma Kelley took a step toward her son, brandishing a fist in his face. "Are you?"

"Step away from us, Ma. The only one threatening anyone is you. You try that again or you put a finger on my wife, and I won't be held accountable for my actions. For someone who is supposedly too weak to walk, you are doing an admirable job standing here making a show of yourself. We should call Reverend Timmons to witness your remarkable recovery."

The crowd laughed as Ma Kelley stared in disbelief at her son. She swung her gaze to Laura, her message clear.

She's an enemy for life now.

"What's all the commotion?"

The crowd parted as the sheriff walked over to them, followed by a smug looking Bertram Shaw. Laura saw Little Beaver stiffen. *He's expecting trouble.*

"Sheriff, you have to arrest that savage. He attacked me. Ida saw everything."

"Yes, sheriff. He put Mrs. Kelley's arm behind her back. Looked awful painful." Ida stopped talking at the look the sheriff gave her.

"Little Beaver, care to explain why you put your hands on a…lady?"

"I only defended myself. She was going to strike me. I cannot explain why, as she called me the savage." Little Beaver took a deep breath before continuing in a serious tone. "Miss Laura took us to the forest to learn how to survive in the wild. This is something the children from my tribe are taught when they are very little. It is to save their lives. Why would this be a waste of time? Do the people of Clover Springs not want their children to be safe?"

Laura noted a few people in the crowd looking guilty and uncomfortable. They seemed to regret being part of the protest. She hoped today was a learning point for everyone. Well, maybe it was too much to hope Mrs. Kelley would change her ways.

"Sounds like a good idea to me." The sheriff glared at Mrs. Kelley. "No doubt Mrs. Kelley would prefer the boys to be taught needlework."

Ma Kelley's face turned so purple, Laura had to hide her face in Paul's chest. She couldn't laugh. Not in front of all these people.

"We went fishing. Didn't catch anything, though. Bertram made too much noise crying for his ma," Peter said, giving the Shaw boy a dirty look.

The crowd laughed again. Laura thought the sheriff was trying hard not to laugh, too, but it was hard to know, as his large mustache was covering his lips.

"Sheriff, Little Beaver is telling the truth." Meggie Petersen pulled at the sheriff's leg. "That lady wasn't nice to him. She was nasty to our teacher, too. She scared me. She called Miss Laura a witch, and she isn't. She's lovely, and I love her, and I want my ma." Meggie's sobs rang out loudly, getting louder as some of the other children joined in.

"Mrs. Kelley, I've a good mind to arrest you for causing a disturbance. Sounds to me like you started this whole thing. You people ought to be ashamed of yourselves, letting this old harpy lead you into devilment. Bertram Shaw, you'll come down to my office and do as many chores as I can think of as punishment for wasting my time."

Ma Kelley looked fit to explode with temper while Mrs. Shaw and Ida Hawthorn burst into loud sobs. Ma Kelley opened her mouth, but the sheriff wagged his finger at her.

"One word from you, and I'll put you in a cell to cool off. Now move along, people. Clover Springs is a nice place to live. We don't hold with people being mistreated due to their race or background. You might want to consider thanking God he sent you a sensible teacher who will look to your child's welfare as well as their education."

The crowd dissipated, leaving Ma Kelley alone with Paul, Laura and some of the children.

"Jenny, take Meggie home, please. Little Beaver and Ben, go with them and make sure they get home safely."

"Yes, Miss Laura."

"You think you've won. Well, you haven't. I'll find a way to get rid of you and then my son will come home. Where he belongs."

"Ma, stop it. I won't ever leave Laura. She's my wife and my future. You were welcome to join our family, but not after today." Paul turned his back on his mother. "Come on, Laura, let's go home."

Laura couldn't look at Paul's mother. She couldn't stand the woman, but that didn't mean she didn't feel her pain at the loss of her son. She may have brought it on herself, but that thought wasn't going to comfort her at night. Laura shivered.

"Are you all right?"

"Thank you for what you did and said." Laura sniffed, trying hard not to cry. She hated showing weakness.

"Laura, you're my wife. I will always defend you. I wish I had a teacher like you when I was young. Going fishing on a school day! That's every boy's dream."

"We didn't just go fishing. It was an educational trip," Laura protested until she saw he was smiling. He was teasing her. Feeling silly, she gathered her things together.

"Are you ready to go home?"

Laura looked up into his face, certain he was asking more than what the words suggested. But what if she was wrong? What if he just felt a sense of duty toward her? What if…

"What?"

His question startled her.

"You looked so pensive there, as if you had a thousand questions on your mind. Is there something you want to ask me?"

Do you really love me? Laura hesitated, trying to put her thoughts into words. But she couldn't. Her nerves were frazzled from the ugliness outside. She couldn't cope if he rejected her, too.

"No, I was just thinking about…Bertram."

"Seriously? He deserves everything the sheriff gives him and more."

"He is only a child. It's his mother who deserves the punishment."

Paul took her hand and drew her toward the door of the classroom. "Maybe, but let's not ruin the rest of our day thinking about the Shaws. Come on, Mrs. Kelley, let's go home."

CHAPTER 31

Paul couldn't bear the look of sadness on Laura's face. He understood that Father Molloy's information about Coleman looking for her had scared her. But it was more than that. She seemed to be retreating back into the shell she had lived in when she first came. The encounter in town led by his Ma hadn't helped.

What she needed was something to look after. He looked at the wriggling bundle in his hand. Being the runt of the litter, nobody wanted him, so Charlie Stanton was going to kill him. Paul had taken one look at the puppy and bought him for Laura. He felt a bit stupid now, as he didn't even know if she liked dogs. Also, he had taken a risk with this one. It was so young and skinny it might not survive. Losing a pet wouldn't help his lovely wife overcome her past.

Pushing the door open, he stopped at the vision in front of him. She'd obviously taken advantage of his plan to go into town and decided to take a bath. He hated to intrude on her privacy, but his legs wouldn't obey his instructions to go back. He watched, mesmerized, as she washed out her hair. He hadn't seen it loose before. He fought the urge to walk over and run his fingers through it. He coughed, hoping she would hear him and realize she wasn't alone. He coughed louder. She jumped, grabbing the towel, soaking it and the floor surrounding the bath in the process.

"You're home. I thought, I mean—"

"I'm sorry. I didn't mean to intrude. I planned on going to town, but then I came across Charlie Stanton. You haven't met him yet. He's not a favorite of Sorcha's, but he's never done me any harm. Anyway, he wanted rid of this little mite and I thought, well—" He coughed to cover his embarrassment. "I got him for you."

"A puppy? Oh, let me see him." Laura was so excited, she seemed to forget she was naked. He turned away, but not before he caught a glimpse of her body. She was gorgeous. The big splash told him she had immersed herself fully in the water once more. He didn't trust himself to look. "I'll take him out to the barn for a quick wash while you get sorted. God only knows what Charlie was feeding him. He's skin and bones. Maybe you could rustle him up some warm milk? When you're ready."

"Thank you, Paul."

"My pleasure." His voice sounded gruff even to him, but he couldn't help it. He had to get out quickly.

"Paul, I thought you were going to the Petersens."

"I was, but then I thought you might like to come along. You could visit with your friends. You haven't seen them in a while." He forgot about the bath and turned back to see her face.

Her smile made leaving even more difficult. But he had to go. He couldn't very well stand there and watch as she got dressed. *She's your wife. Yes, but now is not the time.*

"We can go tomorrow evening if you prefer," he said as he walked toward the door, the puppy squirming in his arms distracting him somewhat from the vision his wife presented.

"No, I would like to go tonight. We can take the puppy with us. Have you given him a name?"

"Blackie, but if you prefer, pick something else."

"No, Blackie suits him. Nobody ever gave me a present as nice before. Thank you."

Her pleasure was evident from her tone. It had a similar effect on him as the image of her in the bath. Embarrassed, he moved quickly to the door. "I'll go get the wagon ready. Will you need long?" His voice was gruffer than usual, but he couldn't do anything about that. He wasn't a saint.

"Only a few more minutes. I'll heat up some milk before we go so Blackie won't be hungry."

Paul almost ran in his haste to get to the wagon and away from temptation. He had promised not to rush her, but even he had his limits.

CHAPTER 32

Laura woke early the next morning and decided to drag one of the old rockers out onto the wooden porch. She had some mending to do and liked to do it outside, weather permitting. Even though she had been here weeks, the view of the mountains still mesmerized her.

The little house Davy had lent them was in need of repair, but Laura didn't care the front door no longer closed snugly or that a few shingles had blown off the roof. She made it as comfortable as possible. It was the first time she had a proper home of her own. Johnny's home was a couple of rooms above a saloon. In the orphanage, she shared a room with Sorcha and Mary. This little house was all just for her and Paul.

Paul worked on the repairs in his spare time. He was kept busy during the day helping on the ranch and building the wraparound porch Davy was installing for Mary. Laura was worried Paul was working too hard, but he didn't seem to mind. He said it kept him occupied. Was he trying to work so hard he could forget about his falling out with his ma? All her life, Laura wanted a family. Even knowing Ma Kelley, she still couldn't understand how anyone could turn their back on their own child. A good man like Paul deserved better.

She cleaned the house until it shone. Paul joked the spiders went running when they heard her skirts rustle. She was pleased with her efforts. Mary had donated a couple of things from the big house—a few cushions here and some rag rugs there. She picked wildflowers every few days so there were always fresh flowers on the table. Her cooking skills were improving, too. Mrs. Higgins was teaching her. The cast iron stove took a little getting used to. Initially, they shared meal times up at the main house, but without discussing it, she realized Paul made excuses to eat at their own table as often as she did.

Paul wasn't much of a talker around company, but with her, he never stopped. He spoke of his dream of having a carpentry business where he would work all day long making furniture and other pieces. He wouldn't have to farm again. Well, apart from helping her weed her little vegetable patch. He liked the idea of living close to town, but far enough away for some privacy. Children need space to run and explore. Then he'd blushed. He still slept on the floor in front of the fire, leaving Laura the bedroom.

She watched Paul as he worked, liking the kindness he showed toward the animals. He was firm but kind, never rough and impatient. She'd noticed from his reaction to things they witnessed in town that he hated cruelty to others, be they human or animals. He hated bullies; hence the reason he had warned her about Bertram Shaw. He told her a little of his experiences growing up as a small boy. His own ma called him the runt of her litter, a nickname that followed him to school, courtesy of his older brother The nickname persisted, even when his body suddenly shot up and he found himself looking down at his brother and his friends. Paul didn't like violence and couldn't be provoked into fighting. He didn't have much time for any cowboy whose horse bore deep spur marks or whose mouth bled from an ill-fitting bridle.

He was a good man, and yet she still hesitated. Her heart raced when he caressed her hair or dropped a kiss on her forehead. She longed to kiss him back, but was that something a good girl would do? She didn't know how experienced he was with women, but he knew she'd been married before.

"It's good to see you smile again."

"I smile all the time," Laura replied as Paul came toward the porch.

"Not really. You haven't smiled properly since Father Molloy's telegram arrived."

Laura didn't want to think of Coleman. He reminded her of her previous life in Boston. She picked up her mending and walked back into the house. Paul followed behind her.

"See, you're frowning again. If you keep looking that cross, the wind will shift and leave you like that forever."

She laughed out loud as he pulled a funny face. He moved a step closer to her, studying her reaction. She didn't move. He must have taken that as a good sign. Sliding his hand under her chin, he forced her to look up at him.

"I'll protect you, Laura. You are safe here. I don't want you ever to feel like you have to do anything. If you want to smile or frown, that's your decision. I am not going to force you to be anything other than who you are." He took a step closer, feeling her breath on his neck.

Her eyes brimmed with tears. One escaped to roll down her face. Using his thumb, he gently wiped it away. She saw his gaze flicker to her mouth before moving back to look directly at her. She wet her lips, as her mouth was dry.

She waited for him to kiss her, closing her eyes, anticipating the touch of his lips. But nothing happened. Stunned, she opened her eyes slightly to see what he was doing. He caught her looking at him, but he didn't move a muscle. It was as if he was waiting for something. But what?

She yearned to move into his arms, to draw them around her so he would hold her close, but she couldn't. It wouldn't be proper. He'd think she was immoral. Yet he was waiting for something. His hand still cupped her chin.

Was he waiting for her? Could she make the first move? What if she was reading this wrong? *Oh, for heaven's sake, Laura, he's your husband. He could force you to fulfill your marriage vows. I have to take a chance.*

Cupping his face in her hands, she leaned up on her tippy-toes and brushed her lips against his. Instead of pushing her away, he pulled her closer against him. His mouth took possession of hers, fierce but gentle, as his hand moved to cradle her neck. His other hand moved around her waist, holding her firmly against him.

Affection surged through her. He was strong but tender. She could feel him holding himself back. He's afraid of scaring me. She moved closer to him, wanting to be close to him.

Their kiss deepened as she shook with emotion.

This was better than she ever believed possible. This is what it felt like when you loved someone. Love.

He broke their embrace, moving quickly away. Shocked, she stared at him as her breath, like his, came in short gasps.

"I'm sorry, Laura. I didn't mean to scare you."

"You didn't."

She wanted to move closer so he would take her in his arms again. Her legs wouldn't move. It was as if she was frozen to the spot. She couldn't understand why he had stopped. She waited for him to explain, but he didn't say a word. Embarrassed at the way she had flung herself at him, she started moving quickly around the little room. She threw her shawl around her shoulders, willing her voice to sound normal.

"It's late and I have to get ready for school. See you later."

She didn't wait for him to answer, but grabbed her basket and moved so quickly out of the house she was almost running. She moved faster when she heard him calling her to wait. She couldn't stop or look back. Her cheeks flaming, she prayed she wouldn't meet anyone she knew on the way to school.

PAUL STARED AFTER HER. She couldn't run away fast enough. What had he done wrong? *You didn't tell her you loved her. Women like to hear those things. Don't they? How would you know? It's not like you're an expert on courting.*

He'd wanted to pick her up in his arms and carry her through to the bedroom, but she wasn't ready for that. Was she? She seemed to enjoy the kisses. He kicked at the floor. He couldn't help thinking he had hurt his wife, even though that was the last thing he intended. Should he go after her? No. Best to give her time to settle down a bit. They would talk later when she came back from town. *Talk.* Maybe it was time for something more than talking. Frowning, he headed for the stables. What he needed now was to get as busy as possible so he wouldn't count the hours until the woman he loved came home.

CHAPTER 33

"Emer, do you mind if I ask you something?"

"No. Why don't we sit down and have some of the pie Mrs. Higgins sent over. I swear I am so fat already, Doc will have to make a new door for the office."

Laura thought pregnancy suited her friend. She was tired, but there was a glow on her face. She couldn't help feeling a little envious of her friend's happiness.

"So what do you want to know?"

Emer's question jolted Laura from her thoughts.

"I wondered, well, why would a man not want to..." Oh, this was no good. She couldn't ask. It wasn't proper. She turned away to hide her scarlet face.

Laura couldn't continue. She felt disloyal to Paul

for even discussing something so private with her friend.

"Paul is a gentleman, Laura. He will wait until you are ready."

"What if that never happens?" the truth burst out of Laura, shocking both of them.

"I thought you liked Paul. From the way you look at him sometimes, I thought real love had grown between you. Don't you feel anything for him?"

"I do, but he's a man."

Emer didn't say anything.

"What I mean is that men don't usually wait. If they like something, they just take it. What if he doesn't like me?"

"He does, Laura. Not only can you see it every time he looks at you, but look at what he did. He married you despite his mother not approving. He left his farm —well, his mother's farm. I don't know him very well, but he's a kind man. He's also shy. He was so sweet when he first came here asking me to find a mail order bride for him."

Laura sat at the table staring into her cup. She couldn't dream of having this conversation with any of the other girls despite the fact that they were her friends. Emer had lived a different life before she came to Clover Springs. She was most likely to understand the life Laura had left behind.

"He knows I was married before. That should make it easier, shouldn't it?" Laura twisted her dress in her hands, her need to know overcoming her embarrassment.

"Paul knows, or he guesses, you weren't treated kindly. I am guessing he doesn't want to do anything to scare you. He may just be waiting for a sign from you. Give it time. You haven't been together very long. It will happen." Emer moved slowly and lowered herself into a chair. "Is he doing anything to make you think he regrets getting married?"

"No, not at all. He brought home Blackie. He takes me on picnics and we go swimming in the creek. He's kissed me a couple of times, but it hasn't, you know, developed."

"Have you encouraged him?"

"Emer, I couldn't do that. He would think I am wanton."

Emer burst out laughing. She didn't stop even when Laura stood up.

"I don't see what's so funny. I'm sorry I even asked. Forget we had this conversation."

"I'm sorry, Laura. I didn't mean to offend you. But you are married. Paul is your husband. It isn't wanton to show your husband some affection. You need to tell him he is welcome to share your blanket."

Her confusion must have been obvious, as Emer explained.

"Nandita uses that term for married couples."

Laura noticed Emer massaging her back. She was also squirming a bit in the chair.

"Emer, are you in pain?"

"It's nothing. It's coming and going. It's too early for the baby. She isn't due for another three weeks or so."

"She?"

"Lawrence decided the baby was a girl. He'll be disappointed if it turns out to be a boy."

Laura didn't comment. She doubted Lawrence Shipley would be upset with anything his wife did. She watched Emer closely. She wasn't an expert on birthing babies, but something told her Emer was closer to having this baby than she was letting on.

"Where's Doc and Mrs. Grey?"

"Doc went to visit Ma Kelley. Yes, again! He has a path worn in the dirt road up to her place. Mrs. Grey will be here in a little while. She went out to check on Sorcha."

"Sorcha is due before you, right?"

"Yeah, she should have the baby any day now. Nandita is staying close. She has a lot of experience birthing ba— Ow, that hurt."

"Emer Shipley, that baby is coming. You're the

nurse. You should know these things."

"I don't know anything about birthing babies. Wasn't much call for it with the Bainstreet gang, and Mrs. Grey wouldn't let me go with her when I was single. Said it wasn't proper. Then she wouldn't let me — Ow. Laura, go get Lawrence, please."

"Lawrence has no place at the birth of his child. I know that much. You better go and lie on the bed. I'll go get Katie. She'll know what to do."

Laura picked up her skirt and ran to the door. She didn't like seeing Emer frightened. The woman was usually so much in control. She opened the door and walked straight into a man's chest. The familiar odor of musk filled her senses. Oh no, he's here. Her gaze moved slowly up as she prayed hard it was someone else wearing the same cologne. But it wasn't.

"Good afternoon, Mrs. Dawson. You took quite a while to track down. Although I must say it was worth it. You are even more beautiful than when we last met." He raised his hand as if to caress her face, but she shrank back from his touch. That angered him. He pushed her back into the office. Two men followed after him.

"Lock that door. We don't want any interruptions. Search the premises. I don't want any surprises," Coleman ordered as Laura moved quickly toward the back exit. "No point trying to escape that way, Mrs.

Dawson. One of my men is standing right on the other side."

Laura stifled a scream. Emer hadn't appeared, but she was in no state to help her. She was alone. She had to play for time.

"What do you want, Coleman?"

"Is that any way to greet a long lost friend?"

"We're not friends. Leave me alone." Laura moved toward the door, but she had only taken one step when his hand snaked around her wrist, pressing it tightly.

"You have spirit. I like that in my women. Johnny said you did, but you didn't show much of it that night in the club. You behaved like a scared rabbit. But then Johnny was known for beating his girls into submission."

Just hearing that name again was enough for Laura to break out in a sweat. Her mouth filled with bile, and she fought the impulse to gag. She had to get them out of here. Emer and her baby were depending on her.

"What do you want?"

"I should think that's obvious," Coleman said, jeering her

"I don't have any of Johnny's money. There was gold in the safe. I don't know what happened to it."

"I don't want money, Laura."

She went cold at the look in his eyes and the tone

of his voice.

"We both know it's you I came for. I intend on taking you back with me to Boston."

"But why?"

He pushed some hair back from her face before stealing a kiss. She gagged in response, causing him to slap her. It wasn't too hard, but the look in his eyes warned her it was a taste of what could come.

"I won't go anywhere with you. I won't leave my husband."

"He's dead."

Laura's stomach lurched. "He can't be." An image of Paul smiling at her that morning filled her mind. *I killed Paul, too.* A lone tear escaped before she swallowed hard. She wasn't going to let Coleman see he was scaring her.

"Didn't they tell you at the hospital? Dawson died the night you got hurt."

Laura exhaled sharply. Johnny. He was talking about Johnny. He doesn't know about Paul. She couldn't tell him. She sensed a wedding ring wasn't going to stop him.

"Boss, we got another one here."

One of Coleman's men pushed Emer roughly toward his boss. Laura watched in admiration as Emer stood up straight.

"I don't know who you are, Mister, but you best

leave here quickly. My husband won't take kindly to any man putting his hands on me," Emer said in a cold but calm voice.

You wouldn't guess she had been writhing in pain minutes before.

"Don't they teach you ladies manners out here? Threatening a guest is no way to behave."

"It's not a threat, but a promise. Get out. Now."

"Who's going to make me? A little girl like you?" Coleman laughed harshly before turning to his men. "She's not my type. Too near to having that baby, but if any of you want her, feel free."

Laura saw Emer blanch at Coleman's words. With a stricken look, she backed away slightly as his men looked her up and down.

"Been such a long time since I had a woman, I don't mind if I do."

Laura watched the scene in slow motion, although everything happened so fast. The man who'd spoken took a step toward Emer. Her friend put her hand in her skirt. Laura thought she was going to run, but instead a loud bang rang out. The man fell flat, blood pouring from his face.

The other men stood stunned, their mouths open at the vision of a pregnant woman shooting their friend. Coleman reacted first. He grabbed Laura and pulled her close to him, using her body as a shield.

"That was a lucky shot, Miss. Put the gun away or my men will kill you."

"A lucky shot? I've been shooting since I was a young'un old enough to hold a gun. You don't know who you're dealing with. Now let Laura go and get out of here while you still can."

Laura's admiration for Emer soared as her pregnant friend faced down Coleman and his gang. She could see the pain in Emer's eyes, but nobody else seemed to have guessed she was in labor. She couldn't hold on much longer. *I have to do something.*

"I'll go with you. Just let Emer go. I've had enough of this small town anyway." Laura forced herself to touch Coleman and look up into his face. "Take me with you, please."

"Laura, no."

"I told you plenty of times, Emer. I don't fit into this town. The women hate me 'cause their men fancy me. I want some fun. I'm too old to be watching every step I make." Laura moved toward the door. "Are you coming or not? We don't have much time before someone comes to find out what the gunshot was."

Coleman was staring at her so hard, she wasn't sure whether he was buying her act or waiting for her to do something. She didn't have any tricks up her sleeve. She just knew she had to get him and his men away from Emer.

"You heard the lady. Come on, boys."

"Boss, what about Mikey and the other lady?"

Laura shot a glance at Emer, who had turned pale and was now holding the pistol in both hands, her knuckles white. Why had the doc moved his office to the edge of town? The bigger premises came at a cost. Nobody was close enough to hear the gunshot.

"Her husband will be here any second. He's the sheriff."

"We don't need any more trouble with the law. Come on, boys, leave Mikey. He's gone." Coleman moved so quickly neither woman saw him. He took the gun out of Emer's hands and knocked her to the floor.

"You got lucky, Mrs. If I had more time, I'd take you with us and show you exactly what happens to someone who hurts my men." With a vicious kick to Emer's side, he moved back to the door, pulling Laura after him.

More men were outside holding some horses. Coleman threw Laura up on a horse before climbing up behind her. And then they were gone. Laura couldn't see anything; the tears streaming down her face were blocking her vision. Would Emer be all right? What about the baby? What sort of man would kick a pregnant woman?

CHAPTER 34

Paul couldn't concentrate. He had a horrible feeling Laura was in trouble. She was late. School had finished two hours ago and there was still no sign. Davy hadn't seen her on the road when he came back from dropping off Mary and Cathy at the Petersen place.

He had no way of knowing what had happened at school. Ben hadn't been in school due to a bad cold and Little Beaver had stayed home to help with some chores.

You're being silly. She can handle Bertram Shaw. She probably made him stand in the corner after class. Maybe he should go drive into town and collect her. He grinned. His wife didn't like it when he got all protective. She had an independent streak. He looked back at his drawings, trying to concentrate on the task at hand, but his thoughts niggled at him. It would be quicker to drive into town and bring Laura home. Then he could concentrate on the job he wanted to complete before sundown.

"I need some more nails. Got to go into town. Need anything?" Paul asked.

"Nails? Now?" Davy looked up, not bothering to hide his amusement. At a glare from Paul, Davy went silent, but his eyes were still laughing.

"Take Little Beaver with you. He's got the attention span of a gnat. Anyone would think it was his wife having the baby."

"Mrs. Petersen is having her baby?" Maybe Laura had been called in there to help. What did Laura know about having babies? He colored at the route his thoughts led him along.

"Come on, Little B. Sooner we get to town, the quicker we will be home to finish our chores."

He decided to take the horses. It would be quicker than the wagon and he liked the fact his wife would have to share his ride. *Getting a bit desperate to hold her in your arms, aren't you?*

Little Beaver went on ahead, seeing as he didn't have to saddle up. He would check the Petersen ranch to see if there was any news on Sorcha and the baby. "If Laura is there, can you tell her I am heading to town?"

Paul rode off to some good-natured jesting from Davy. He knew his boss hadn't swallowed his excuses, but he didn't care. As he rode, he thought about Laura. It was driving him mad living in such close quarters to her but not being able to make theirs a real marriage. He was trying to be patient, but Dear Lord, how long would it take his wife to trust him? He couldn't bear to do anything to hurt her, but at the same time, he was so in love with her. He wanted nothing more than to feel her arms around him, to run his fingers through her glorious hair. He loved everything about her. She was spirited and brave as well as intelligent and kind. Sure, it took her a while to open up to people, but given what she'd been through, that was expected.

Little Beaver caught up with him just as they had the town of Clover Springs in their sights. "Baby hasn't come yet. Nandita sent Brian off on a long walk with Frank. Said us men were getting in the way."

"Was my wife there?"

Little Beaver shook his head, his gaze focused on the town. Paul looked, too. It seemed busier than usual outside the doc's office. Was someone hurt? Laura. He urged his horse on faster, barely allowing the animal to come to a stop before jumping off. He threw the reins at Little Beaver before walking up to the sheriff. He dimly noticed a hush fell on the crowd, but before he could react, a woman's scream rent the air.

Laura? No, that wasn't her.

"Mrs. Shipley is having her baby. Doc's in with her now."

"Is everything okay?" Paul could see the sheriff was worried. He knew the man was a bachelor, but surely childbirth wasn't that scary.

"Paul, we got trouble. Mrs. Shipley's been beaten up and Mrs. Kelley is missing."

Ma was missing. How? Not Ma. He was talking about Laura.

"Paul, did you hear me, son? Your wife's been kidnapped. Miss Emer shot one of the men before she got hit."

"Where is he? Ask him what they want with Laura."

"He's dead, Paul. Reckon those men didn't know Emer was a crack shot. Pity she didn't get all of them."

"How long have they had Laura? We've got to get after them! What are you standing around here for?"

"Calm down, Paul. We don't know for sure who has her and what they want. They didn't take anything else, not even her bag. Miss Emer said Laura seemed to know the man, so I'm guessing it's the Boston gang. But that doesn't help us much. We don't know where they went."

"I can track them."

Little Beaver moved forward, his gaze on Paul. "You know I can do this, Mr. Kelley. My father taught me well. I want to help Miss Laura. She's been kind to me."

"Appreciate your help, son, but you aren't old enough to join a posse."

"Let him, sheriff. He knows what he's doing. I don't care about anything other than getting my wife back."

CHAPTER 35

Laura gave up fighting back. She had kicked and bit Coleman one too many times, resulting in a backhanded slap, knocking her out. When she came to, she didn't recognize her surroundings. Tears of frustration smarted in her eyes. Why couldn't he leave her alone? She had a life in Clover Springs with her friends. With her husband. Paul. Oh, please God, don't let him come after me. Coleman will kill him. Let him forget about me.

She closed her eyes, the image of Emer lying helpless and curled up on the floor. She prayed hard her friend and the precious baby she carried would be all right. Surely Doc or someone had come to the office and found her. She wriggled and twisted, but the rope securing her was too tight. She couldn't reach the knot. That didn't stop her, though. She kept working at it long after her fingernails bled from the chaffing.

"No point in trying to get them bonds loose, girl. I tied them up real good."

Laura held herself as still as possible as he pawed her. He held her chin roughly as he forced her to look up at him. She spat at him. "Spirited filly, aren't you? I am looking forward to breaking you. I thought Johnny would have done that already."

"I'm nobody's filly. Now let me go."

"Can't do that, Miss Laura Lee. You and I got business waiting back in Boston. That pretty head and mind of yours is going to make me a fortune."

Laura tried her best to hide her terror. She couldn't go back to Boston, to that life.

"I won't work for you. I'm done with that life."

"You will work for me. I ain't asking you. I'm telling you. Johnny cost me a packet. As his wife, you owe me." He looked her up and down. "It's a debt I am looking forward to collecting."

Her fingers itched to slap the leering look off his face.

"Never," she hissed. His response was to slap her once more.

"You'll learn. Girls like you always do. I never lose."

"Boss, we got to keep moving. That girl you kicked, turns out she's the wife of one of the richest men in town." Laura peeped through her eyelids. She recognized the man speaking to Coleman. He was a regular at the store. Always smelled to high heaven, making most people give him a wide berth. But he was talking about Emer. Was she all right?

"Her old man is connected to Shipley bank. They're rolling in it, Boss. He's offered a reward for you, 100 dollars dead or alive. The whole town seems to have joined the posse."

"And you thought you'd grab the money for yourself by leading them here, did you?"

The man paled, visibly shaken by the threatening tone. "Course not, Boss. I came here to warn you. You told me to stay behind."

"Course you did." Coleman smiled at the man, whose relief was obvious from the look on his face. It didn't last long before the knife slashed through his chest.

"I didn't tell you to meet me here, did I? Chances are you led them right to us."

The man gurgled something, but Laura couldn't make out what he said. She watched in horrid fascination as the man died. Coleman calmly cleaned the blade before turning back toward her. She closed her eyes, hoping he'd believe she hadn't seen what just transpired.

He wasn't Johnny. He was far more dangerous.

"Sorry you had to see that, Lee. I like to protect my girls from the more sordid side of life."

"I am not your girl. I'm a married woman and my husband will come get me." Even as she said the words, Laura was torn between wanting to be rescued and not wanting to put her husband in danger. She loved him.

THEY RODE HARD the next day. Coleman wouldn't let the men make a campfire. He didn't want the smoke alerting anyone to their whereabouts. The men complained about the cold meal. Coleman released her bonds so she could eat. At first she was tempted to throw the meal in his face, but one look at his eyes told her he was expecting that reaction. Instead, she forced herself to eat the food. The mixture of uncooked corn meal, water and molasses made her want to gag, but she needed to keep her strength up. She was going to escape one way or another. She was not going to betray Paul with this man.

"Where we going, Boss?" one of the men asked Coleman. "Seems to me like we're heading in the wrong direction if we're aiming to go to Boston."

"Who said we're going back to Boston? That's exactly the direction the posse will take."

"But you told Jed and Sam to meet us in Denver."

Coleman's eyes glistened dangerously at the belligerent tone the man had used. The man coughed and spat into the ground, not backing down from the challenge.

"Jed and Sam know they were to create a diversion. I don't discuss every decision I make. Now you got any more questions?" Coleman's hand rested on the pearl handled revolver sticking out of his belt.

Still, the man ignored the signs. Laura wondered if he couldn't see in the darkness or he was just so wound up and liked playing with fire.

"So where we going then?" The man's tone was slightly less challenging this time.

"There's a mining town further up the mountain. We will lie low there for a couple of days. There's plenty of entertainment for you boys. I will be busy entertaining our guest." Coleman winked at Laura.

Oh no you won't. She didn't react but pretended she hadn't understood his meaning. She sensed he was disappointed. *So he likes baiting me.* She had to think of a way to slow them down. If they got to the mining town, they would be able to hire guns. There were always those unsuccessful miners who would do anything for a few dollars. Coleman put a rug on the ground for her to sleep on. He tied her legs loosely together but her hands were bound more tightly.

"Sit tight and get some sleep. We will be riding hard tomorrow."

He kissed her hard on the lips.

"I can't wait to find out what had Johnny smiling so much."

Laura had to swallow hard not to vomit, but she didn't want to anger him.

"I'm going to scout ahead, but don't try anything. Billy has orders to shoot anything that moves, including you, my dear."

Billy raked her with his eyes, earning a clip around the ear from Coleman.

"She's mine. You don't lay as much as a finger on her, you hear?"

"Yes, Boss. Sorry, Boss," the man mumbled, rubbing his head.

CHAPTER 36

Coleman was leaving camp for a couple of hours. This was her chance. She had to escape. She closed her eyes until she sensed he had left. She couldn't run, as her legs were bound. How could she get away? She couldn't. But she could try to send a signal to the posse she hoped was tracking them. She had to start a fire. But how?

The ground was dry. Little Beaver had taught the school children how to make a campfire using only stones and some dry leaves. She closed her eyes, remembering the lesson. It had been part of her plan to encourage greater communication and trust between the children. She felt around the ground with her hands. It was difficult with them being bound, but at least Coleman had bound them in front of her rather than behind. Billy hadn't taken long to start snoring—obviously thinking she was going nowhere.

She moved slowly, not wanting to alert him. She worked at the rope using her teeth to help make it looser. She couldn't remove it completely, but it got loose enough to let her move her hands some more.

Using her feet, she pushed together some leaves, twigs and anything else she could reach, thanking God it was so dry. If she could make a spark and her prayers were answered, it shouldn't be difficult for the flame to catch. She kept one eye on the sleeping form of the man who was supposed to be watching her.

Taking two stones, she rubbed them together. The grinding noise sounded so loud she was sure it would wake Billy or bring someone else, but it didn't. Billy grunted a few times but didn't wake up.

It wasn't working. She had to try harder. Biting her lip, she rubbed the stones together harder. Her skin was chaffing, but she ignored the pain. She had to do something. She would die before she'd let Coleman or anyone else touch her. Anyone but Paul. Closing her eyes, she thought of her sweet, kind husband. Why hadn't she told him she loved him? Why had she stayed in town to talk to Emer instead of going home and showing her husband how much she cared for him? By waiting, she had put Emer and her baby in danger as well as blowing what might have been the only chance for her to show Paul how grateful she was.

Angrily brushing the tears from her eyes, she worked the stones harder. A spark. One spark. That was all she needed. Billy grunted again, but it wasn't that sound that made her work harder. It was the tremor on the ground made by horses' hooves. Coleman and the others were coming back. This was her last chance.

She prayed hard. One spark quickly followed by another and some of the bundle in front of her started to smoke. She blew on it, trying to fan the flames. Sweat poured down her back as the noise of the returning horses came closer. She blew again and again, rubbing the stones harder now. Nothing mattered now but making the fire. The flame caught just as Billy woke up. He shouted at her, but in his haste to get up, he fell over his own feet. She kept going, fanning the flames and piling on some green leaves as they produced more smoke than the dry kindling. The flames took hold much quicker than she believed possible.

"Put out that darn fire. What did I tell you about building a campfire?" Coleman's voice preceded him.

Billy pushed her away from the fire forcibly, causing her to fall backwards and jarring her arm. She screamed as loudly as she could. If it hadn't been so dangerous, she would have laughed at the look on Billy's face. He couldn't make up his mind whether to gag her or put the fire out. She kept screaming as he kicked dirt over the fire, trying to douse it.

"Don't throw water on it, you fool!"

Before Coleman could stop him, Billy threw his canteen of water on the fire, causing smoke to billow in all directions. She'd done it. Even if the posse didn't see the smoke, they would find traces of the fire when they came looking for her. *That's if they come this way and don't follow the false trail Coleman set up for them.*

Coleman slapped her a few times, but she kept screaming until he pulled out his pistol and held it to her head. She didn't care if he shot her. He seemed to read her mind as he turned the gun on the hapless Billy.

"Shut up or I'll kill him."

Laura stopped screaming. She didn't like the outlaw, but she couldn't be directly responsible for a man dying.

"What in the blazes were you thinking of? I told you to watch her."

Billy opened his mouth, but he didn't get a chance to say anything.

"Clear the camp now. Everyone mount up. We got to get away from here now."

Coleman pulled Laura roughly to her feet. She

shrank back from him as he held his face close to hers. “I’ll enjoy making you pay for that little stunt. Just you wait.”

She couldn’t stop her mind reliving some of the ways Johnny had made her pay for past mistakes. Shivering, she forced herself to breathe slowly and deeply to work her way through the dizziness. She wasn’t going to black out from fear. She had to use her emotions to strengthen her resolve. She had promised not to let another man use her that way again. It was a promise she intended to keep regardless of the consequences.

CHAPTER 37

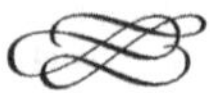

"Those tracks are as plain as day. They are headed to Denver." Charlie Stanton got back on his horse.

"No, they aren't. They want you to think that. It is too obvious."

The sheriff rubbed his jaw. Paul looked from Charlie Stanton to Little Beaver.

"Stay here. I won't be long."

Before anyone could say anything, Little Beaver had raced off in the direction of the tracks.

They all watched him for a few seconds before the sheriff spoke.

"What do you think, Kelley? I know your wife was afraid of some men from Boston, but I'm inclined to agree with the Indian. Those tracks are mighty clear for a group of men trying to hide."

Paul didn't know what to think. He itched to be moving, not standing here. He couldn't help thinking of what could be happening to Laura all the time they were waiting around. But it wouldn't make sense to ride off in the wrong direction. Shouts broke into his thoughts. Little Beaver came racing back.

"Those tracks are only two horses and two riders. If they had Miss Laura, one horse would be making stronger tracks carrying a heavier load. It's a…what do you call it?"

"A ruse? They are trying to get us to follow these tracks?" the sheriff asked.

"Yes, sir. That's exactly what they are trying to do."

"Sheriff, are you going to take the word of a boy? This is the first strong lead we got since leaving town. I think we should go this way," Charlie Stanton protested loudly.

Paul looked at the other men in the posse, some of whom seemed to agree with Charlie. He saw the anger on Little Beaver's face, although the Indian did his best to hide it.

"Sheriff, I say follow Little Beaver. It seems mighty convenient those tracks are so clear. A little too helpful."

"I agree, but I can't force any man to follow me. If you men want to follow Charlie, go now. But be careful. They could be leading you into an ambush. The rest of you follow us. Little Beaver, we are right behind you."

Little Beaver sent a look of thanks to Paul before riding off. Some of the men broke away to follow Stanton, but the majority fell in behind the sheriff. Paul looked in the direction Little Beaver was taking. It headed straight into the mountains. Where on earth were the kidnappers taking Laura?

They rode hard, but not as fast as Paul wanted to move. He closed his eyes, picturing Laura as he had last seen her. She'd been laughing as she told him about her lesson plans for the day. He'd ached to kiss her properly, but instead he had simply grazed her forehead with his lips. He thought sometimes she was ready to become his wife in every way, but then other times she still looked scared.

He'd been patient. She was the love of his life. His woman. He'd sworn to protect her and look at how that had ended up. His stomach heaved as he thought of what she might be going through now. His fingers gripped his gun, thinking of how much he wanted to put a bullet into the men who had taken her. He, who hated violence, now wanted to rip their heads off and feed them to the ants.

Up above, Little Beaver had jumped off his horse once more. He walked for a while, gazing intently at the ground. Paul rode up near to him.

"Can you see anything?"

"I think so, but I wish my grandfather was here with me. He is a much better tracker than I am."

"Your grandfather trained you well, Little Beaver. Have faith." *Please hurry.* Paul bit down on his impatience, knowing the boy was doing his best. It wasn't going to help Laura if he threw him off his work by demanding he move faster.

"This is a puzzle. For a while now, we have been tracking one horse."

"One? What on earth?" Was Charlie right all along? Why would the Indian track only one horse when it was a group that took Laura?

"Yes, one horse with one rider moving very quickly following four other horses. But now there are only four riders and one loose horse."

"What are you saying? Another diversion?"

"There's blood on the ground. It's fresh." Little Beaver didn't look at Paul, but continued to scrutinize the ground closely.

Paul fought not to go racing off ahead. Blood? Was it Laura's? Had they decided to dump her to throw them off? He gripped his reins so tight, his knuckles gleamed. Little Beaver sent him a glance of sympathy before running off in the direction of some trees. Paul made to follow, but the sheriff stopped him.

"Let him go. Some sights a man shouldn't see."

"You think it's her, don't you? She's dead."

"Paul, you and me both know a good woman like Laura might think that was the preferable option. Don't go looking at me like that. We don't know whose blood it is."

Paul tried to keep a grip on his temper. It wasn't the sheriff's fault he was putting Paul's thoughts into words. Every man and woman in Clover Springs would be thinking the same thing. Why else would a woman be kidnapped? Oh, why hadn't he acted on his impulse and kissed her properly that morning? Made her stay home from school. Kept her safe with him. *Because she isn't a prisoner and you are not her jailer.* She loved that job. Loved being a teacher. Don't go writing her off now. She's a fighter. Look at what she had already survived.

"Paul."

His gaze followed the sheriff. Little Beaver was coming back. He had something in his hand.

"It wasn't Miss Laura. It was a man. He was wearing this."

"Joe Duffy had a scarf like that. Was it him?"

"I don't know this Joe Duffy. He's dead, though. His body is up in those trees. Looks like they dragged him over there."

The sheriff rode in the direction Little Beaver indicated, followed by a couple of men. He came back alone. "It was Joe Duffy all right. The men are going to dig a grave for him. Wonder what he was doing out here?"

"Know him well? I can't say I remember him."

"Bit too well. He's a drinker, so he landed in the cell a few times. Nothing serious, though. He was relatively new to town. Said he came down from one of the mining towns when his luck gave out."

Paul couldn't concentrate on what the sheriff was saying. It wasn't Laura. She was still alive. Up there somewhere. He looked toward the mountain. Someone had lit a fire. It wouldn't be the group they were looking for, since they'd know the smoke would be seen.

"Do you see that? Looks like a small fire. Maybe some hunters. They might know something."

"Won't hurt to ask. We're going that direction anyway, aren't we, Little Beaver?"

Little Beaver nodded, but his face wore an expression Paul couldn't decipher.

"What?"

"Could be nothing."

"Tell me. Please."

"I think that fire could be Miss Laura. I taught her how to make a fire in class. See how much it smokes? Hunters wouldn't make so much smoke." Little

Beaver's cautious excitement was contagious. "I think Miss Laura is trying to send us a signal."

Laura was using smoke signals. Was there anything his wife couldn't do? Laura wasn't going to let this gang beat her, so neither was he.

"Come on, men, my wife is up there."

Renewed with hope, the men rode harder than they had before despite the difficult terrain. They soon came to the site of the fire. As Little Beaver had said, it was too small to be an effective campfire. As if to prove it, Little Beaver jumped to the ground and picked up something. He handed it to Paul.

"It's from Miss Laura's dress. She was here."

Paul grinned at the Indian. Laura was alive and leaving tracks for them to find her. He was filled with wonder and awe for the bravery his wife was showing.

"We must be more careful now. They are not far ahead. We don't want them to hear us coming and kill Miss Laura."

The sheriff nodded.

"What do you suggest we do, Little Beaver?"

"We should leave the horses here with one or two of your men. I will take my horse. She is more familiar with tracking. She won't make as much noise."

The sheriff dismounted, despite the muttering from some of the posse. Paul hopped off his horse too.

"I'm going with you."

"You should stay with the horses. I don't want doc to have to dig any more bullets out of you."

"Sheriff, that's my wife out there. I'm going with or without you."

"We must move as silently as possible. The trail is difficult for their horses, so they will not be moving quickly either. We will catch them soon."

The men filed into a line behind the sheriff, who followed Little Beaver as they climbed up the mountain. The Indian walked beside his horse, examining the ground closely. They moved as silently as a band of cowboys could. Soon they heard some horses, the sound coming from further up the mountain.

"We need to spread out. If we continue as a group, we are a bigger target." The sheriff ordered the men to split off into twos and threes. Paul stuck as near as he could to Little Beaver.

"Miss Laura is still alive, Mr. Kelley. See, she leaves patterns for me to find."

Paul looked at where Little Beaver was pointing, but he couldn't see anything. It just looked like a couple of leaves. But the boy seemed to read something into it, so he had to take his word for it. His mind couldn't contemplate a life without Laura.

CHAPTER 38

Laura forced herself to take shallower breaths. The further they got up into the mountain, the more difficult breathing became. She continued to pick leaves as often as she could, dropping them after her. She didn't know how much longer they would keep riding. She felt Coleman stick his spurs into his horse again, her heart breaking for the poor animal. Coleman was an idiot. The horse couldn't go any faster, given the rough terrain.

Laura strained her hearing, hoping to hear someone giving chase, but the valley and forest behind them yielded nothing. Did Paul know where she was? She prayed, even though it didn't seem like God was listening. But he had to be. Father Molloy said God never denied anyone who was in trouble. If being stuck up a mountain with a gang like Coleman's wasn't trouble, Laura didn't know what was. *But you got yourself into this mess. If you hadn't been so eager to marry Johnny, you would have seen him for what he really was.* Laura kicked herself mentally. It was pointless thinking about the past.

She had to find a way to slow their progress. Out of the corner of their eye, she saw Coleman was preoccupied. She looked around her. The terrain was slightly less rough than before. There were fewer rocks. She wanted to hinder their progress, but she wasn't quite ready to kill herself yet. Taking a deep breath, she whispered a quick apology to the horse before kicking it. The animal reared in surprise, throwing Laura and Coleman off the mount just as she had planned.

They both hit the ground with a thud, although Coleman got the worst of it, breaking her fall in the process. Her elbow jarred as it hit a rock. *Thank goodness it wasn't my head.*

"What did you do that for, you stupid woman? You could have killed the both of us."

Laura didn't answer but pretended to have lost consciousness. She hoped it would make her heavier to carry as Coleman struggled to get back on his feet. Praying valiantly, she fell over a few times, pulling him back to the ground as they tried to find their footing. At some point during their struggles, her gag fell loose, allowing her to spit it out. Breathing heavily, she allowed herself time to enjoy the freedom from the smelly gag.

"Enough. I'm getting tired of your games. I will put an end to this right now."

She heard the click as he pulled the hammer back.

"Go on. You might as well kill me. I'll never do what you want. Never," she screamed at him, her voice echoing through the mountains.

"Boss, shut her up. They'll hear us miles away."

Laura kept screaming despite the gun waving in her face. *I don't care anymore. Paul isn't coming. There's no way out. I've had enough.*

CHAPTER 39

Little Beaver stopped as they all heard the screams.

"Laura. That's Laura."

Before Paul could shout, Little Beaver put his hand over his mouth.

"They do not know we are here. Do not lose the element of surprise. Keep quiet. Miss Laura's alive. We are close."

Paul fought hard against his desire to scream back, telling Laura they were close. He knew Little Beaver was right. If Coleman and his gang thought they were cornered, it would make them more dangerous. Like a wounded grizzly.

So he sat and waited for Little Beaver to scout ahead. He came back within a matter of minutes, although it seemed to take hours.

"What took you so long?" Paul knew he was being testy, but waiting was killing him. His mind kept going to where it shouldn't. Imagining Laura suffering.

Little Beaver shrugged his shoulders. He waited for the sheriff to join them. "There are four men. One has a gun pointed at Miss Laura. She seems to have upset him."

Paul went to move, but Little Beaver restrained him.

"We cannot go rushing in. There is no way to protect Miss Laura. We have to plan this better. We need to tell Miss Laura we are close."

"How do you plan on doing that, son? It's not like we can just call out to her and pray Coleman's lot don't hear us."

"I can signal to Miss Laura. We practiced it at school."

"Didn't you just learn math and English? I didn't do any of this when I was at school." The sheriff pulled at his whiskers. "I don't have any better ideas. Do you, Paul?"

Paul shook his head. He couldn't get his tongue off the top of his mouth. Laura was so close, yet she might as well be in Boston. He wanted to race to her rescue.

"You must think with your head and not your heart, Mr. Kelley." Little Beaver's look surprised Paul. It seemed the boy understood more than he let on.

"What do we do?"

"You wait. I will signal to Miss Laura. Hopefully she will move away from the men. I will move to her side as soon as I can. Then you will attack."

"How will we know when you are ready for us, son?" The sheriff asked.

"This is your signal."

Little Beaver mimicked the sound of an owl so well, Paul found himself looking up to the sky before realizing the stupidity of his actions. The boy was clever. And he was gone.

CHAPTER 40

Laura stared down the gun barrel. She bit back her panic. She didn't want to die, but this was preferable to a future with Coleman. She waited for him to pull the trigger, but he seemed to be finding it hard to shoot a woman. She opened her mouth to antagonize him when she heard the bird call. It was the sound of a cuckoo. The signal that help was near. She forced herself to look directly at Coleman when every instinct was telling her to search the surrounding woods looking for Little Beaver.

"So are you going to shoot me? If you aren't, I need to..." Laura gestured in the direction of some trees.

"Don't push me, lady. If I didn't have serious plans for you, you wouldn't be still alive."

"I'm sorry. Johnny was always telling me my

temper was my downfall. I'll try and behave, but I really need to go." Laura despised the weak little girl's voice, but she'd try anything to get away. He continued to stare at her. She couldn't make out what he was thinking. "Please. I really am desperate."

"Go over there. Not too far and don't try anything funny. I've had enough of you. There are plenty of other pretty girls out there."

Go find one of them then. Laura didn't reply but half walked, half crawled toward the clump of trees he had pointed to. She moved behind one, hoping he would think she was looking for privacy. She waited, but not for long.

A hand came down over her mouth before she was picked up like a bag of potatoes and carried off. Her heart pounded despite recognizing Little Beaver's scent.

As soon as he put her down, he cupped his hands together, making a loud owl sound. The sounds of guns exploded around them. Laura cowered in fear, even though the fight was behind them. Little Beaver used his knife to free her hands. Then, taking one hand in his, he pulled her along as he ran off. She followed as quickly as she could, but the combination of her long skirt and hours without proper food and drink slowed her down.

"Come on, Miss Laura. Mr. Kelley's going out of his mind worrying about you."

Paul was here. She picked up her skirts and ran faster, ignoring the push of her lungs. He was here.

"Laura, where are you?"

She heard his voice, but it seemed to be coming from behind them. They slowed as Little Beaver did his bird call whistle again. "Miss Laura, we'll wait here. Hide just in case that man comes. I will track back to see."

"No, don't leave me alone. Please."

"Miss Laura, you will be fine. It's nearly over. Be brave a little while longer."

She stood staring after him, but he looked back and motioned at her with his hands. She crouched down to hide. She strained her ears; the shooting seemed to have stopped, but she couldn't hear anything. Was Paul okay? *Please don't let him have gotten hurt. Please, Dear Lord, don't take him away from me.*

"Laura, where are you? Come out. It's safe. Coleman's dead. His men are with the sheriff."

Laura stood and stared as Paul ran toward her. He grabbed her into his arms, wrapping her into his embrace, his kisses raining down on her cheeks. His tears mixed with hers.

"Darling, I'm so sorry. I should have been there."

"I'm sorry too. Is Emer okay?"

"Emer is fine. The doctor was seeing to her when we left. No doubt she'll have a baby to show us when we get home."

Laura stilled. Home. Did he still want her? After everything?

"What? Are you cold? Do you want my jacket? Shall I carry you?"

"Do you still want me as your wife? You know what type of man Coleman was. Why he wanted me?"

"I don't give a cow's behind what he wanted. You're mine, Laura, my wife, and I don't intend ever letting you forget that."

She rose up on her tippy toes to land a kiss on his lips. "You promise?"

"Yes, Mrs. Kelley, I promise. Just as soon as we get home, I am going to show you just how much I love you."

"Oh, Paul, I love you, too. With all my heart and mind."

"That's some mind you got, darling. Little Beaver showed me the trail you left for us. You are one clever lady."

"Little Beaver." With one last kiss, Laura moved away from Paul and walked toward where the Indian and sheriff were standing. "I owe you my life. "

"No, Miss Laura. You did most of the work. You made it easy for me."

"You showed me how to make a fire in the wilderness and what the Indians look for when tracking an animal. I just put what you showed me into practice."

"Thank God you did. That Coleman was a nasty piece," Sheriff replied.

Paul came up behind Laura, putting his arm around her waist, drawing her close.

"He killed one of his own men right in front of me. Didn't even think twice about it." Laura shuddered, causing Paul to pull her closer.

"Yes, we know. Thanks to him, we hit your trail." The sheriff turned to Little Beaver. "Come on, son. You can teach this old dog some of your tricks. Let's leave the love birds to it."

Paul and Laura watched the old sheriff and the young Indian boy walk away. Paul pulled Laura closer to him, kissing her thoroughly.

"Laura, don't ever leave me again. I don't think I could handle life without you."

"I'm not going anywhere. Not without you. Take me home, husband."

EPILOGUE

ONE MONTH LATER

"It's true then. You are alive."

Laura flinched at the woman's tone.

"Ma. I told you before. Leave my wife alone." Paul stood closer to Laura, holding her hand tightly in his. She squeezed his hand in thanks.

"You're not coming back to teach school. You are not a good influence on the children. They deserve better than a…"

"Mrs. Shaw." Reverend Timmons spoke sharply, causing the woman to flush. "Mrs. Kelley, Laura, I speak for the entire town when I say we are delighted you have agreed to come back to teach school. We hope you have recovered from your ordeal."

"Thank you, Reverend. I feel much stronger now. I am more than ready to come back to work next Monday."

"Thank God. I was worried when Katie Sullivan told me her sister had decided to stay in Boulder. I had visions of having to teach school the whole time. I have to say, teaching doesn't come naturally to me. The children can be quite a handful at times, but dealing with some of the parents has really tested my patience."

Laura and Paul laughed as the Reverend rolled his eyes.

"Reverend, I object." Mrs. Shaw puffed out her considerable chest as she spoke.

"Oh, please do not worry, Mrs. Shaw. You weren't the only parent I found difficult to please. Now, if you will excuse me. Mrs. Timmons and I are going on a picnic. Perhaps you would like to accompany us?"

He directed the question to Laura.

"We would love to, Reverend, but I have things to get in the store. I want to make sure Katie isn't too upset about Ellen's decision. Thank you for the invitation. Enjoy your afternoon."

The Reverend tipped his hat before walking off in the direction of his home.

"Come on, Mrs. Kelley, let's go see the sheriff. Good afternoon Ma, Mrs. Shaw."

Laura had to hold her breath not to laugh at the expression on their faces.

"Paul, your mother is never going to accept me."

Paul stopped walking to take his wife in his arms. "Paul, stop it. We are in the middle of town."

"I don't care where we are. I love you, Mrs. Kelley, and if Ma can't see that, she can go swim in the creek." Laura smiled at that image. Paul brought his face so close to hers, his forehead was leaning against hers; she struggled to breathe. "I nearly lost you, Laura. I am not afraid to admit it. I thought I would never see you again."

"Are you two lovebirds coming inside, or do I have to arrest you for public disorder?"

"Ah Sheriff, can't a man kiss his wife?" Paul joked as they walked into the jailhouse.

"You keep the kissing business to your home, where it belongs. Now. Sit down. I have something serious to tell you."

Laura's heart sank. *Coleman was dead. There couldn't be any more trouble coming for her, could there?*

She reached for Paul's hand as they both took the seats indicated by the sheriff. He sat opposite playing with his whiskers as he chewed his tobacco.

"Mary told us you wanted to see us but she didn't know why. Tell me Sheriff, please."

"I said it was serious, Miss Laura; I didn't say it was bad news." He smiled, showing his yellow stained teeth.

Laura glanced at Paul but her husband was staring at the sheriff.

"Little Beaver did a mighty fine job of tracking you, Miss Laura. I don't mind admitting we could have lost you if it weren't for that boy."

"Yes, Sheriff. We are both very grateful to Little Beaver."

This time, Paul looked at Laura. She could see her confusion mirrored in his eyes. What was the sheriff trying to say?

"The lessons he gave your students also helped a lot. Wouldn't you agree?"

"Yes Sheriff." Laura leaned forward. "I intend to spend more time teaching the children basic survival skills. Little Beaver has said he would be delighted to help."

"Yes, well that may cause me a slight problem." The sheriff coughed before rolling his tobacco chew to the other side of his mouth. Laura glanced at the spittoon, wondering why he didn't use it. *Perhaps he is trying to treat me like a lady.*

"I went out to speak to Frank and Nandita. They are as close to guardians as Little Beaver has. They agreed, with some persuasive talking on my part, to allow Little Beaver to come work for me."

Laura sat back in her chair. Paul looked as stunned as she felt.

"That's a wonderful idea, but isn't he a bit young?" Laura asked.

"Well, I'm hoping you orphans are done with keeping this old sheriff busy," the sheriff smiled. "I will train Little Beaver on the law and, in turn, he will train me how to track."

"I think that's the best idea I've heard in ages, but won't some of the townsfolk be upset?" Paul commented.

"You leave me to worry about the townsfolk. Now, there is something else. It's a little delicate. It involves Miss Laura's past."

Laura's heart beat faster. She waited in silence, aware of her husband looking at her in concern.

"Seems there was a certain amount of gold in your dead husband's safe. The police have closed their investigation into his death." He looked at Laura, but she couldn't respond. "This means your dead husband's personal effects have been released."

Laura stood up so quickly the chair she had been sitting on fell over. "I don't want anything to do with him. Tell them to give it to someone else."

"You might not want to be so hasty." The sheriff picked up some papers, handing them to her. She crossed her arms, not wanting to touch anything linked to Johnny. Paul stood up to take the papers. He gave them a quick read before he sat down quickly.

"Two hundred dollars."

"The gold and other cash in the safe was a little more, but some costs had to be covered. Burial and such."

"I don't care how much it is. I don't want any of it. That's blood money."

"I see this has been a shock. Perhaps you should take Miss Laura home. You don't have to make a decision today."

Paul shook the sheriff's hand before wrapping his arm around her waist. She was grateful, as her legs seemed to be walking through mud. She opened her mouth to say something to the sheriff, but the words wouldn't come.

"Come on, Laura, let's go home."

* * *

The ride home passed in silence. *Why does he have to come back and ruin things? He's dead and he's still trying to control me.* She glanced at Paul a few times but the look on his face stopped her from speaking. He looked disgusted. *Was he sorry she'd been rescued? It would have been better for everyone if Coleman had killed her.*

They pulled up outside their little house. Laura was thankful nobody saw them. She jumped down from the wagon, ignoring Paul's attempt to help her. She couldn't deal with anything other than the images in her head now. She wasn't taking the money. It was tainted and would only bring bad luck.

* * *

Paul took his time seeing to the horses. He hated seeing his wife so upset. She was only just recovering from the kidnapping ordeal, and now this. He wished the money had disappeared. Why did the Boston police have to contact the sheriff? Would Laura ever be able to leave her past where it belonged—the past?

He walked slowly into the house. She wasn't in the kitchen. Pushing open the bedroom door, he saw her lying curled up in a ball on the bed. She was crying.

"Laura, darling. Don't cry."

"I'm so sorry. I know you are angry."

"I'm furious, but not at you. Darling, you are not to blame. The police are only doing their job. The money belongs to you."

"I don't want it. It's dirty. Do you hear me? That money came from the devil himself." Laura was almost screaming. "He's still controlling me. After all this time, he can still reach me."

He pulled her into his arms, ignoring her half-hearted resistance. He hadn't let Coleman or his ma keep them apart. He wasn't going to let a ghost do it either.

"Laura, darling. I love you. Nobody controls you. You are free. You and I have a happy future ahead of us. Johnny and Coleman are dead. They don't have the power to hurt us anymore. Not unless we let them. "

Laura stopped crying, angrily rubbing the tears from her eyes. "I am letting him in again."

"You aren't. You got a shock today. That's all."

"I don't want his money." Laura looked into his face, the look of horror in her eyes fading slightly. He pulled her closer, kissing her deeply.

"I love and respect you, Mrs. Kelley. Whatever decision you make, I will stand by your side." She smiled tentatively. He kissed her again. "Don't make any decision now. Think about this, Laura. Maybe you could use the money to do something good. To wipe out some of the harm Johnny and his friends inflicted on our world."

"Something good? Like what?"

"I don't know, exactly. Maybe write to Father Molloy and ask him. Or ask Katie and the other girls. There has to be a way to put that money to help God's work. Think about it, darling. It could be your revenge. Using Johnny's ill-gotten gains to help some unfortunate."

"He'd hate that."

"He doesn't exist anymore. He's gone."

Paul kissed her again, his embrace deepening as her body responded to his passion. He loved this woman more than life itself. Sometime later, they lay curled up together. He caressed her shoulder.

"I love you, Mrs. Kelley."

"I love you too Mr. Kelley. It's wonderful being married. I can't understand why anyone would choose going to university over having a family and a home."

"Mmm, what?" he said, distracted.

"Oh you! Poor Katie—she was looking forward to having her sister back in town."

"Mrs. Kelley, I love you, but can we stop talking about your friends? It's a little distracting." He nuzzled her ear.

"Anything you say, husband. After all, I promised to obey you."

"You did, didn't you?"

He tickled her, his heart soaring at the sound of her laughter. Whatever life threw at them, they would deal with it. Together.

Thank you so much for reading Laura. I hope you want to continue reading about her and her friends in Clover Springs. Ellen, the next book brings back old friends and introduces new ones.

ALSO BY RACHEL WESSON

The Resistance Sisters

Darkness Falls

Light Rises

Hearts at War

When's Mummy Coming

A Mother's Promise

WWII Irish Stand Alone

Stolen from her Mother

Orphans of Hope House

Home for unloved Orphans (Orphans of Hope House 1)

Baby on the Doorstep (Orphans of Hope House 2)

Women and War

Gracie under Fire

Penny's Secret Mission

Molly's Flight

Hearts on the Rails

Orphan Train Escape

Orphan Train Trials

Orphan Train Christmas

Orphan Train Tragedy

Orphan Train Strike

Orphan Train Disaster

Trail of Hearts - Oregon Trail Series

Oregon Bound (book 1)

Oregon Dreams (book 2)

Oregon Destiny (book 3)

Oregon Discovery (book 4)

Oregon Disaster (book 5)

12 Days of Christmas - co -authored series.

The Maid - book 8

Clover Springs Mail Order Brides

Katie (Book 1)

Mary (Book 2)

Sorcha (Book 3)

Emer (Book 4)

Laura (Book 5)

Ellen (Book 6)

Thanksgiving in Clover Springs (book 7)

Christmas in Clover Springs (book8)

Erin (Book 9)

Eleanor (book 10)

Cathy (book 11)

Mrs. Grey

Clover Springs East

New York Bound (book 1)

New York Storm (book 2)

New York Hope (book 3)

ACKNOWLEDGMENTS

This book wouldn't have been possible without the help of so many people. Thanks to Erin Dameron-Hill for my fantastic covers. Erin is a gifted artist who makes my characters come to life.

The ladies from Pioneer Hearts who volunteered to proofread my book. Special thanks go to Nancy Cowan, Marlene Larsen, Cindy Nipper, Marilyn Cortellini, Sherry Masters, Janet Lessley, Robin Malek, Meisje Sanders Arcuri and Denise Cervantes who all spotted errors (mine) that had slipped through.

I'd love you to come hang out with us at my readers group on Facebook at https://www.facebook.com/groups/rachelwessonsreaders

Last, but by no means least, huge thanks and love to my husband and my three children.

Made in the USA
Las Vegas, NV
15 November 2023